FOR LOVE OR MONEY

FOR LOVE OR MONEY

Joanne Lennox

CHIVERS

British Library Cataloguing in Publication Data available

This Large Print edition published by BBC Audiobooks Ltd, Bath, 2007.
Published by arrangement with the Author

U.K. Hardcover ISBN 978 1 405 64040 4
U.K. Softcover ISBN 978 1 405 64041 1

Printed and bound in Great Britain by
Antony Rowe Ltd., Chippenham, Wiltshire

CHAPTER ONE

As the aeroplane cruised thousands of feet above Asia, on its way to Thailand, Emma Lombard closed her eyes and tried to get some sleep. She'd never been good at sleeping in public places, though, and matters weren't helped by the man sitting to her right, clattering away on the keys of his laptop computer. Eventually, frustrated, Emma's brown eyes flickered open and she sighed heavily.

The man glanced across at her.

'Sorry,' he commented drily, raising an eyebrow. 'Was I disturbing you?'

He made to close the lid of his laptop, and instantly, Emma's kind-hearted nature made her feel guilty.

'No, no, you go ahead.' She sighed. 'I can never sleep on aeroplanes anyway.'

Wide awake now, she couldn't resist sneaking a peek at the screen of the laptop. The screen was dense with text, although Emma caught sight of the word, PRIMATE in a sub-heading, before the lid of the laptop was snapped shut.

Jumping sheepishly, Emma glanced up at the man, who met her gaze, the faintest hint of a grin curving the corners of his mouth.

1

'Sorry,' she muttered again, a curl of wavy brown hair flopping over her face. 'That's another of my failings, besides not being able to sleep on aeroplanes. I can never resist reading other people's newspapers over their shoulders, and I suppose laptops amount to much the same thing. It's a terrible habit.'

The corners of the man's dark eyes crinkled in ironic amusement.

'Don't worry,' he said. 'You weren't missing much. It was tedious stuff.'

By now, Emma's mind was working overtime. Primates—that referred to monkeys and things, didn't it? That didn't sound particularly tedious to her. Still, if she'd hoped for the man to enlighten her further about his intriguing document, it seemed she was going to be disappointed. And she was disappointed. Already she could sense something mysterious about this man, as if he had a secret, and that, with her inquisitive nature, made her want to know more.

'I'd hate to stop you working,' Emma said, with a smile. 'I promise I won't peek again. I'll keep my eyes fixed on the spectacular view out of the window.'

'It's OK, thanks,' he replied and glanced at his wristwatch. 'We're due to land in about half an hour. I wouldn't get much more done now anyway.'

There was a couple of minutes' silence between them, broken only by the soft snoring of the businessman sitting to the right of Emma's companion in their row of three seats. Emma concentrated on the view from the small window, on the tantalising flashes of exotic land and sea barely visible through the clouds.

'So,' the man said suddenly, startling Emma out of her reverie, 'what brings you to Thailand? On holiday, are you?'

Emma's wide mouth couldn't help curling into a secretive smile.

'I'm a woman,' she said teasingly, 'so you immediately assume I'm visiting Thailand in search of idle pleasure. Is that it?'

The man raked a hand through his dark brown hair, looking chastened.

'I apologise,' he said evenly. 'That was an arrogant assumption to make. I'd like to think I was usually more intuitive about people than that. So, are you going to put me right?'

'I'm a businesswoman,' Emma said, with some pride. 'I'm visiting Bangkok hoping to source some interesting luxury or ethnic items to sell in my shop.'

Ironically, her sales assistant and best friend, Alison, had urged her to treat the week-long trip as a vacation.

'You're due a holiday anyway,' Allie had insisted. 'Go on, make a trip out of it. The business is doing so well, you can afford it, and if you manage to source some good, reasonably-priced stock over there, it'll

3

probably end up saving us money in the long run.'

'A shop?' the man beside her asked now, in that calm, understated manner of his. 'How interesting. May I ask you what sort of shop it is?'

'Exclusive, top-of-the-range gifts, with an international flavour,' Emma clarified. 'It's called Gifted Hands, and it's in the Lanes, in Brighton. You know the sort of thing?'

'It's a pretty exclusive area. I don't live that far from Brighton myself.'

Emma noticed, however, that he didn't volunteer the information as to where he did live. Curiouser and curiouser, she thought. He looked mid-thirties, compared to her twenty-five years, but she didn't know anything about him, not even his name. Hopefully, though, she could put that right.

'Emma Lombard,' she introduced herself, wriggling awkwardly in the seat and stretching out a hand.

He took the hand, his grasp warm.

'Dan Fitzgerald,' he replied.

Encouraged by the achievement of discovering his name, Emma continued conversationally.

'So, er, Dan, are you travelling to Thailand on business, too?'

Now it was his turn to tease her.

'Just because I'm a man, you immediately assume I'm on some macho, go-getting business trip, rather than taking a well-earned break?'

Emma's cheeks flushed, but before she could reply he continued.

'Actually, you're right, Emma. I've got some business to look into in Bangkok. I'm staying at the Indira Hotel, near the Chao Phraya river, as a matter of fact. How about you? Where are you staying?'

At this point, Emma was forced to admit, rather sheepishly, that she didn't, as yet, know.

'This whole trip was rather last-minute,' she confessed. 'I thought it would be just as easy to sort something out when I landed. Although, now that I'm nearly there, the thought is seeming a little more daunting.'

'You could do worse than the Indira. I stay there whenever I come to Thailand. It's well-suited, excellent facilities, and the prices aren't as extortionate as you might think.'

'OK, thanks,' Emma said thoughtfully, considering. 'I might just do that.'

Just then, they were instructed to fasten their seatbelts in preparation for landing. Emma realised she still didn't know anything about Dan Fitzgerald's business.

'So, um, Dan, what are your plans for the rest of the day?' she probed. Dan glanced at his watch again.

'Well, it'll be mid-afternoon by the time I get settled in at the hotel. By then there won't be time for much more than a nap and a shower before dinner, then an early night.'

Once again, Emma felt she was being fobbed off.

'And tomorrow?' she pressed, tilting her head inquiringly to one side. Dan sighed heavily, looking at her.

'You ask a heck of a lot of questions, don't you, Emma?' he commented, though his tone was laced with gentle amusement. 'Very well, if you must know, tomorrow, I'm planning to visit a market.'

'A market?' she echoed, intrigued, and before she could stop herself, she added, 'That sounds right up my street.'

She hesitated, not wanting to be pushy, or force her company on this man.

'I wonder—I mean, would you mind terribly if I came along, too? It's just that, unlike you, I'm not a particularly frequent traveller.'

The corners of his mouth curved.

'Despite your show of bravado about being a go-getting businesswoman, you don't really know where to start, do you?'

The remark was delivered teasingly.

'No! I didn't mean that at all.'

Then there was a silence that seemed too long, but something, maybe the flash of vulnerability Emma hadn't meant to reveal, must have got through to the man, because then he said slowly, reluctantly, 'OK. Have it your way then. I'll take you to the market with me tomorrow, if that's what you really want.'

'There's no need to be like that about it,' Emma said, with a trace of huffiness. 'Don't worry. I don't want to tag along where I'm not wanted. And I can assure you I don't normally throw myself at strange men like that.'

Dan's steely expression relented.

'I can assure you that no man would willingly turn down the recreational company of an attractive woman. But I'll warn you, it's unlikely to be the sort of market you're interested in, for your shop at any rate,' he added.

'Emma furrowed her brow. 'Why's that?'

'It's an animal market.'

'Oh.'

Emma had never been to an animal market before, but she imagined it to be something like a kind of a large pet shop. So this man's business definitely had something to do with animals, then.

'That's OK,' she replied equably. 'If you're sure you don't mind me coming, I love animals. And I could do with a recreational day tomorrow, to get over the flight. I can get down to some serious business the day after that.'

'Fine. I'll look forward to it,' Dan Fitzgerald said, but Emma noticed that he was observing her with a funny look and she couldn't help wondering why.

The following morning, Emma was uncertain exactly how or why she had allowed her business trip to become quite so entangled with the activities of Dan Fitzgerald who, until the previous day, had been a complete stranger to her. She was even wondering if it had been a mistake to share a taxi from Bangkok Airport to the Indira Hotel with him and secure a room in the same hotel in which he was staying. Still, she couldn't fault his recommendation. The hotel was excellent, just as he had promised.

Now, at the appointed hour of ten o'clock, Emma waited in the glass-enclosed, white marble lobby for Dan to show up. She felt refreshed by a good night's sleep, and by a delicious breakfast of exotic fruit salad.

At a minute past ten, a voice said, 'Morning, Emma,' and she glanced up from the magazine she had been flicking through. 'Sleep well?'

Dan's now-familiar, enquiring face met her gaze. Heavens, he was tall, and his stature was even more impressive than she remembered.

'Good morning.' She smiled back, steadying herself. 'In answer to your question, yes, thanks.'

He, too, looked refreshed, since they had parted at the reception desk the previous afternoon, all traces of the stubble shadowing his jaw now removed. Emma felt her heart lift a little at the sight of him.

'You look smart,' he commented, eyeing her tailored, pale cotton trousers and co-ordinating, loose white shirt as she stood up. 'Are you sure you're ready for this?'

Emma gave a brisk nod, and quickened her stride to match his, as he made his way out through the hotel's revolving doors, into the hot, humid day.

On reaching their destination, Emma soon realised this was no ordinary pet store. After a stuffy taxi-ride across the city, Dan had taken her inside an unprepossessing-looking building, to a large, brightly-lit indoor market. Cages and tanks were everywhere, crammed into the relatively small space, and people milled about, shop assistants and prospective customers. Emma's soft brown eyes filled with compassion for the many animals and birds she could see.

Dan turned to her, observing her intently.

'I did try to prepare you, Emma. It's a completely different culture over here.' He went on in a low voice, 'And buying and selling animals is an integral part of that culture. You saw those puppies for sale on the street corner, didn't you, through the taxi window just now?'

Emma nodded, wondering how Dan could sound so detached, cool-headed about it.

'Yes, and snakes in cages.'

She gave a small shudder.

'Until this morning, I wouldn't have

9

thought I could feel sorry for a snake.'

Emma glanced at the market around her, starting to wish she hadn't come.

'Come on,' Dan said. 'Let's have a look around.'

He led her towards some cages containing some parrots, and she followed obediently. The parrots were a beautiful shade of green, with a touch of vibrant orange on their faces.

'They're gorgeous,' Emma couldn't help admitting, gazing through the bars of the cage.

'Eclectus parrots,' Dan informed her. 'Originally from the wild in Papua New Guinea. And those,' he said as he pointed to the neighbouring cage, 'are grey parrots, from Africa.'

'Are they rare?' Emma asked, still staring at the birds.

'Not as rare as the blue and macaws. They come from South America. Fetch about a thousand US dollars each.'

Emma gasped.

'But you won't see them. I suspect they've got some hidden in those cardboard boxes on the shelves up there, because they're illegal.'

'You certainly seem to know a lot about it.'

'Let's just say I've been here before,' Dan said succinctly.

Emma glanced suspiciously across at him, wondering why, unlike her, he didn't think it was cruel to snatch these birds from their natural habitats, to cram them into cages and boxes in this stuffy market place.

They moved on to peer into a murky tank. Dan adjusted his black courier-bag.

'That's a Radiated Tortoise,' he said, close to her ear. 'They're a protected species, too.'

Emma shook her head, muttering, 'I can't believe this place.'

She followed Dan, past a tank full of yellow fish, at which a couple of other tourists were gazing, towards a large enclosure near the back of the market, full of monkeys. He approached a woman shop assistant standing beside a cage, and pointed to the sleepy, monkey-like creature inside the enclosure.

'Excuse me, madam, is that a squirrel?'

The Thai woman smiled indulgently and shook her head.

'No, sir, it's a slow loris.'

Emma gazed at Dan in bemusement. What was going on? One minute he was sounding like the biggest expert on wild animals since David Attenborough, the next he was mistaking a slow loris for a squirrel! Even she could have told him that creature was no squirrel. But Dan was still doing his dumb act.

'May I see?' he was asking, coy as any tourist.

The assistant undid the back of the cage and took out the creature, swinging it deftly round on her arm before handing it to Dan. The slow loris, rudely awakened, seemed to cringe away from the bright overhead light.

Considering Dan didn't know what a slow loris was, he seemed curiously unintimidated by handling one. Emma gazed at the small, woolly brown creature as Dan held it, and its soulful, dark-ringed eyes gazed across at her. Suddenly she could bear it no longer.

'Poor thing!' she gasped involuntarily. 'Oh, put it back, Dan, please! I don't think it likes the bright lights.'

Dan glared across at her, concern etched on his brow. Then he turned away.

'Thank you,' he said politely to the assistant, handing the creature back as he then turned back to Emma. 'I can see you're not too happy. But do you think you could just bear with me for a few more minutes, Emma? Only there's some business I need to attend to.'

Emma glanced imploringly up at Dan.

'All right then, as long as it really is just a few more minutes.'

'Promise.'

Emma knew she'd had enough of this place, and yet she was strangely compelled, when Dan led her onwards and two baby orang-utans in the next cage caught her eye.

'Oh, poor little things,' she murmured. 'Don't they just look so vulnerable? Just like human babies!'

'Orangs like these come from Sumatra and Borneo,' Dan explained gently. 'But they're growing increasingly rare. At the current rate of decline, in ten years time, the only orang-utans left will be on show, not in the wild.'

He spoke calmly, and Emma wondered why Dan didn't sound as outraged or indignant about this as it made her feel.

A Thai man materialised next the cage. He exuded an air of greater authority than the shop assistant.

'Can I help?' the man asked Dan courteously.

Dan pointed to the baby orang-utans.

'How much?'

The man named a figure in the Thai currency, and Dan made a rapid mental calculation.

'That's roughly two and a half thousand pounds,' he explained, turning to Emma, who stifled a gasp.

'How quickly could I get hold of one of these animals?' Dan asked the man.

Emma jerked her head round to look at him, wide-eyed.

'If you want one quickly,' the man continued, speaking in a low voice, in heavily-accented English, 'if you wish to order one today, the orang-utans are more expensive just now,' and he named another figure in local currency.

'Why's that?' Emma blurted out, unable to stop herself.

The man hesitated, giving Emma a wary look before replying guardedly, 'Because a meeting is due to be held in the city in the next few days. The traders are concerned. They would rather not sell the animals till after the conference is over.

'Well, thank you very much for your assistance,' Dan told the man, who was now giving them a look of thinly-disguised suspicion. 'I won't order today, as I can't afford the added cost at the moment and I'm in no hurry. But I will definitely get back to you. What is your name, please?'

'Lek,' the man replied, after a moment's hesitation.

'I'll be in touch, Lek.'

Dan smiled back. Then, grabbing Emma unceremoniously by the arm, he dragged her away, out of the market, back on to the busy, Bangkok street.

Emma banished the feeling that they'd made a narrow escape. She snatched her arm away from Dan's grasp and glared up at him, chestnut eyes blazing.

'Excuse me! What on earth do you think you are doing, Mr Fitzgerald, manhandling me like that? And were you serious about ordering one of those poor little orang-utans?'

Dan glared back at her, equally exasperated.

'I told you to let me do the talking, Emma!' His dark eyes were uneasy. 'Your over-active

14

tongue could have got us into serious trouble back there. And, as for what I said about ordering an orang-utan in the future, well, I had to say something, to get us out of there fast.'

'But I wanted to ask what the meeting was for.'

'I know what you wanted to ask. For your information, the conference has been called to discuss the illegal trade in exotic animals in this country. Rather a sensitive subject, as far as our friend back there is concerned.'

'Well, thank goodness someone intends to do something about the plight of those poor animals!' Emma exclaimed. 'It's barbaric, that market!'

'I knew you wouldn't like it in there,' he muttered. 'I did try to tell you, Emma, but you insisted on coming with me.'

'What about you?' Emma shrieked, so that Dan raised a finger to his lips, in a gesture imploring her to keep her voice down. 'Don't you think it's outrageous?' she continued, more quietly.

'They're desperately poor, the men and women who deal in these animals,' Dan replied calmly. 'For many of them, it's their only way of making money. You can't simply judge it from a Westerner's point of view.'

'Why are you trying to justify this illegal trade?' Emma asked, incredulously. 'It's almost as if you've got a vested interest in the whole business!'

Her voice subsided into silence as her mind continued to work overtime. If her suspicions were true, it was a very unpleasant realisation about this man whom she had come to like. But, despite his protestations of innocence, it was the only explanation that made sense— that Dan Fitzgerald was himself a dealer in exotic animals. He was looking cagey now, but his next words confirmed her fears.

'Let's just say I've got a professional interest in this business,' he said slowly, looking her straight in the eye.

Suddenly, the crowded street, the humid heat of the air around her, Dan's revelation, was too much for Emma.

'Excuse me,' she said faintly. 'I've got to get away. Need some space.'

Dan didn't question this. Stepping forward, Emma miraculously managed to hail a taxi almost instantly. As the taxi pulled up beside the pavement in front of her, Emma opened the door, sliding thankfully on to the back seat. Before she slammed the door, she gave one last glance across the pavement at Dan, who was watching her with concerned, dark eyes.

'Emma, would you let me explain?' he called across towards her.

Tears of emotion welling in her eyes, it was all Emma could do to shake her head reproachfully at him before she pulled the taxi

16

door shut.

'Where to, madam?' the driver smiled at her.

'The Indira Hotel, please,' she said, but, at that moment, she couldn't really have cared where she was going.

Dan stared after the taxi until it disappeared from view, swallowed up in the seething mass of traffic. Then he thrust his hands into his pockets, shaking his head regretfully. He'd known it was a mistake, bringing Emma along this morning, and she'd asked so many questions, she'd almost blown the deal completely. Not that he'd been too impressed by what he'd seen today, either. Still, he had to deal with these people, on a professional basis. But, nonetheless, what he'd seen had been alarming.

By feigning ignorance of the slow loris's true identity, he'd sought to give the impression that he was a mere tourist, and yet the assistant had willingly allowed him to handle the animal, despite the fact that the slow loris had a semi-poisonous bite, and shouldn't have been handed to the public at all. Of course, after the sale the teeth were cut out to prevent this risk, but then the area became infected and the loris wouldn't survive long once it had gone to its new owner.

Dan sighed, and set about hailing a taxi for himself. The events of that morning had certainly given him a lot to think about, and his casual acquaintance with a British tourist should have been low on his list of priorities. So why did he keep seeing Emma's face, as it had gazed at him reproachfully from the taxi, tears welling in those soulful chestnut brown eyes?

CHAPTER TWO

The following day, by the afternoon, Emma was feeling slightly better. The plight of the animals, particularly the baby orang-utans, was still preying on her mind, but she'd managed to distract herself for a few hours, walking the vibrant streets of Bangkok, browsing amongst its air-conditioned plazas and its markets and street stalls, on the lookout for goods to stock her boutique.

Emma negotiated her way through the hotel's revolving doors, carrier bags containing goods and samples grasped firmly in each hand.

'Blast!' she muttered, one of her bags banging her shin as she tried to squeeze through the door.

'Allow me,' a deep voice behind her said.

'Dan!' Emma exclaimed, seeing the man behind her.

Despite their acrimonious parting the day before, Emma couldn't help feeling pleased to see Dan, and gladly relinquished a couple of her bags to him. 'Had a good day of retail therapy, I take it?' he asked.

'Yes, thanks.' Emma smiled back tentatively, as they emerged into the cool marble foyer. 'I found the most gorgeous, hand-painted silk pictures. I'll have them framed at home,' she enthused. 'I also picked up some exotic jewellery over in Chinatown, quite reasonably priced, studded with chips of rubies and sapphires, and I got some small jade buddhas, mounted on teak.'

Dan nodded his approval.

'No wonder you're so laden down. Still, should go down a treat with the punters back in Brighton.'

Dan pressed the button for the lift, and they paused, setting down their bags, waiting for it to arrive. A sudden silence fell.

'Which floor?' Dan asked politely.

'Three,' Emma replied.

'I'm on two,' Dan commented, continuing the mood of courteous civility. 'Room Two, Two, Two, actually,' he added conversationally. 'Even I can remember that one.'

Emma would have liked to maintain a dignified silence as they waited, recalling their falling out yesterday, and her suspicions of the man, but her enthusiasm got the better of her.

'I got talking to the jewellery shop's manager today. He spoke excellent English, and he was telling me that the riverbeds in Thailand sometimes conceal small shards of ruby. Local farmers pan for rubies in the hope of a little extra income. They use wooden sieves to dredge the gravel at the bottom of the river. Imagine how thrilling it must be to glimpse a sparkle of red amongst the stones!'

'And do they find many?' Dan asked,

20

interested, as the lift doors slid open, and they stepped inside.

'The manager said that rubies are rarely found, but if they are discovered, large gems can sell for huge amounts of money. You told me the Thai people had to find whatever ways they could of making money,' Emma murmured. 'It seems you were right.'

'Hey, don't beat yourself up about it,' Dan said mildly, as the lift started its smooth ascent. 'You have helped local businesses today by dealing with the Thai trades people. And, come on, admit it, you're delighted with your purchases, aren't you?'

'I am,' Emma admitted. 'I must phone Allie tonight. She's my assistant and friend, of course, and she'll want a progress report.'

The lift bell pinged as they arrived at the second floor.

'This is me,' Dan said. 'Or would you like me to help you carry those bags to your room?'

'No,' Emma said hastily, too hastily and added, with a smile, 'I think I can manage to stagger two hundred yards unaided, thank you.'

'Point taken.' Dan grinned back. 'You're an independent lady.'

There was a brief pause after the lift doors had slid open, and Dan leaned the heel of his hand on the button.

'Emma,' he began, 'I really am sorry about

yesterday.'

'Me, too,' Emma heard herself saying, returning his gaze.

It was true. She couldn't help liking Dan, and was reluctant to believe that he really was an illegal animal trader. It struck her, too, not for the first time, what an attractive man he was. She felt a flush rise to her cheeks.

'How about a pre-dinner drink in the hotel bar tonight?' Dan suggested, as if on impulse. 'Just to show there's no hard feelings?'

'OK,' Emma found herself agreeing. 'See you there, about seven?'

Dan nodded his agreement, and disappeared down the hotel corridor. It was only after he had gone and the lift continued its ascent that Emma realised that she still didn't know any more about this enigmatic, intriguing and, despite everything, strangely likeable man.

Having phoned Alison and given her that update, Emma vowed to find out more about Dan Fitzgerald and his business, over their pre-dinner drink. Conversation flowed easily between them.

'Do you mind if I join you for dinner?' Dan asked as they finished their drinks.

'Of course not,' Emma replied.

It seemed so natural that she was surprised he'd even felt the need to ask. It was not until they'd finished their meal that she realised she had still failed to turn the conversation to Dan himself. She cast about in her mind desperately for a way of steering the conversation on to the desired subject.

'So, what are you doing tomorrow?' she asked, trying to sound casual.

For a moment, Dan didn't reply, just stared at her across the small table, in a way that made her tingle with awareness. She'd freshened up in her room earlier, put up her hair and dressed for dinner in a halter-neck printed cotton dress, but now, suddenly, her bare, bronzed shoulders felt curiously exposed. Dan himself had made an effort, too, in a more formal shirt and trousers than usual, his dark hair slicked back with a touch of gel.

Eventually, still looking at her, he replied, 'Oh, a bit of this and a bit of that.'

'Sounds fascinating,' Emma replied wryly, taking a sip of coffee.

She paused, wondering how to frame her next impulsive words. She didn't usually come on to men in this way, in fact her last boyfriend, Mark, had made all the moves towards her. But then, this wasn't a come-on, was it?

'The thing is, I was wondering, if you weren't particularly busy, if you'd like to do something together, maybe go on a river cruise to see some temples, or take a trip to the beach?'

There was another, this time slightly awkward, pause.

'I'm sorry,' Dan said finally, coolly. 'I'd like to, but I really can't. I've arranged to meet a business associate. I'm over here on business, not pleasure, after all.'

Stung by his rejection, when they'd been getting on so well, Emma pushed her half-drunk coffee away from her.

'Fine,' she said, getting to her feet.

Enough was enough. She was fed up of his caginess.

'Well, in that case, Mr Fitzgerald, thanks for your company this evening, but I won't take up any more of your precious time,' she stated and then walked briskly out of the bar.

'Hey, Emma, wait.'

Dan caught up with her just inside the entrance to the bar area. Emma remained turned away from him, but he grasped her shoulders, spinning her round to face him. Then suddenly he lowered his face to hers and kissed her.

After some time, Emma broke away, startled by the passion that had flared between them.

'What was that for?' Emma asked him, her soft brown eyes imploring. 'I'm confused, Dan, the way you keep blowing hot and cold, and despite this mysterious business of yours you keep referring to, I still know virtually nothing about you!'

'I will tell you about my business, Emma, I promise. Soon. Look, Em, how about we do something together the day after tomorrow? I've got something in mind, a way of mixing business with pleasure. Although, no, on second thoughts, maybe it's not such a good idea, seeing as you found the other morning at the market rather upsetting.'

By now, however, Emma was intrigued, despite herself. She quickly banished any qualms she might have.

'No, I'd like to come along,' she said firmly. 'I won't wimp out, I promise.'

*   *   *

'Where are you taking me?' Emma asked Dan, as the breezy, open-topped bus headed out of Bangkok the following afternoon.

'You'll find out soon enough,' Dan said mysteriously.

Emma thought that he seemed slightly tense, as he adjusted the black courier-bag on the seat beside him.

'What do you keep in that bag? The crown jewels?' Emma asked.

'You sure ask a lot of questions,' Dan replied, but there was a teasing light in his eyes, and he brushed Emma's hand with his fingers.

The bus finally rumbled to a halt outside an unassuming cluster of wooden buildings a short distance out of the city. Emma gasped as she scanned the letters picked out on the grassy bank in front of them.

'Pakburi Tiger Zoo?' she read incredulously.

'Don't be put off. It's something I feel you should see. Come on.'

Getting to his feet, he took her hand and led her off the bus. He paid their admission and Emma followed him reluctantly through the turnstile.

They wandered amongst the leafy avenues of the zoo, pausing to gaze at the many enclosures of tigers along the way. Inside one of the enclosures, an attendant was feeding a cub milk from a bottle, surrounded by a small group of onlookers. Emma and Dan did not stop to watch but continued on.

'How many tigers have they got here?' Emma breathed disbelievingly.

'Over four hundred I believe,' Dan told her coolly. 'As well as some chimpanzees and orang-utans.'

Stopping suddenly outside a cage, Emma turned to Dan.

'I'm sorry, but I just have to ask. Why exactly have you brought me here?'

'I'll explain soon,' he promised, his dark eyes meeting hers. 'But first, there are some more things I want you to see.'

With that, he led her off the beaten track, down a path that was not signposted. They came to some small pens, and Emma gasped.

'Oh, my goodness. Now that is truly bizarre!'

In each of the row of small enclosures lay a fat pink sow, suckling a small tiger cub. Next to each tiger cub lay a pale pink piglet, wearing a stripy coat of what looked like tiger-print fur fabric.

'If it wasn't so odd,' she murmured, 'I hate to say it, but it would be cute.'

'Strange, isn't it?' Dan said from beside her. 'They bring in sows to suckle the tiger cubs.'

'But where are the tiger cubs' mothers?' Emma asked, wide-eyed.

'Performing in the circus show, maybe.'

His expression was unreadable as Emma turned indignantly to him. 'Is that all you can say? Don't you care?'

'Of course, I care,' he said calmly. 'But that doesn't mean I can solve all the world's problems at the drop of a hat.' Dan glanced at his watch. 'It's five to three now. The board by the entrance said there was a show at three o'clock.'

He grasped Emma's hand.

'Come on. If we're quick we won't miss the beginning.'

'I'm not sure I want to see . . .' But Emma's attempt at a protest tailed off, as she docilely allowed Dan to drag her along.

Her thoughts were churning as she wondered what Dan's business was, not to mention what sort of man he might be.

On the way to the circus arena, they passed a stall selling tiger bones for medicinal purposes, proclaiming them to be a miracle cure for all sorts of ailments. Once again, Emma felt her indignation rising.

'So is that what happens to the old tigers?' she asked Dan.

'Quite possibly, yes,' Dan replied in a low voice as they paused briefly at the crowded stall. 'And why not make a positive out of a negative? Even tigers die of old age, you know.'

'Yes, I do know that,' Emma commented. 'But it still seems a bit distasteful.' She couldn't believe Dan's attitude, not just towards the bones, but generally. She'd wanted to believe that he was better than this.

'In fact,' Dan continued, 'stalls like the one here may be how a zoo such as this makes most of its money. It's a cultural thing, too. The Thai people in particular believe in the healing properties of tiger bones.' He paused. 'As a nation, they abhor cruelty as much as we do. Anyway, come on. We don't want to miss the show.'

'Don't we?' she muttered, as he led her along.

When they got there, the tiered concrete arena was humid and busy, but Dan still found a couple of empty seats not too far from the front. There was an announcement in Thai, and then one in English.

28

'Ladies and gentlemen, please take your seats. The three o'clock show is about to commence.'

Emma and Dan watched as tigers performed a number of tricks, culminating in a huge, magnificent male jumping through a flaming hoop. Despite her disapproval, Emma was horribly mesmerised by the visual spectacle, as applause rippled around the arena. The second part of the show consisted of young orang-utans and chimpanzees performing various tricks.

Emma saw that Dan was staring at one particular young female chimpanzee, incongruously dressed in a yellow cardigan and tutu.

'What are you looking at?' Emma murmured, curious in spite of herself.

'That chimp over there,' Dan replied in a low voice, leaning his head confidentially towards hers. 'I couldn't help noticing. Her face looks deformed.'

Following his gaze, Emma saw that Dan was right.

'Her face is all swollen, poor little darling,' she breathed, her eyes filling with tears. 'You can hardly make out the features.' It was heartbreaking. 'You know, Dan,' Emma said suddenly, her voice rising with emotion, 'I really don't know why you've brought me here. What's the point in seeing this suffering, when we're powerless to do anything about it?

I know I said I thought I could handle it, and I've stuck it for as long as I can, but I think I've seen enough now.'

The last of her words were almost drowned as applause broke out around the arena as the show ended, and the chimpanzees, orang-utans and their trainers took their final bows. Dan did not join in the applause, but stared at Emma, saying nothing. Almost apologetically, he reached over and gave her hand a brief, sympathetic squeeze. In spite of herself, Emma found herself mollified by the gesture.

'Well, at least that's over,' she went on, steadying herself as the applause finally subsided, and the arena started to empty. 'Maybe we can leave now.'

'I'm sorry, Emma, but I can't leave just yet. I've got to stay and talk to someone. It shouldn't take too long, if you don't mind waiting for me.'

'Dan,' she exclaimed frustatedly, 'I've had enough of this place. I just want to get out of here!'

'If that's what you want,' Dan said quietly, 'you shouldn't have any trouble getting back. I believe there's a bus along every twenty minutes or so. Just take care, won't you?'

Something in his tone almost made Emma relent. Instinctively, something made her reluctant to believe that he was a bad man.

But she said softly, reproachfully, 'And this trip was supposed to be part-pleasure as well as part-business? Excuse me, but the pleasure part of it seems to have escaped me.'

'For me, the pleasure was in your company,' Dan replied simply.

Then he turned on his heel and hurried off down the arena steps, towards the circus ring, leaving Emma to make her way up out of the arena, through the zoo, and back towards the bus-stop.

As Dan strode purposefully towards his intended destination, his mind was buzzing. Why oh why did I ever get Emma involved in this, he thought to himself. He was usually a pretty level-headed bloke. Had he put her in a dangerous position by doing so? But, no, he reasoned. If they'd got into any trouble, he'd swear her innocence in all this, explain how they'd met for the first time on the plane over.

Dan spotted one of the animals' trainers, lurking about towards the back of the circus ring, gathering up some of the props, but even as he made towards the man, still his own mind was working overtime.

Why was I so bothered about Emma seeing this place today, he asked himself. Because she's come to mean something to me in a couple of short days? Because, for some reason, her opinion matters?

The Filippino trainer heard his approach, and turned towards him with a bemused smile.

'Can I help, sir?'

Dan smiled in what he hoped was an

unthreatening way.

'Yes, please. I'd like to talk to you about one of your young female chimps. She looks to me as though she's got some sort of infection in one of her teeth, and I believe she may need antibiotics.'

Arriving back at the hotel an hour later, Emma felt more confused than ever. Dan seemed a nice man, he even seemed to care about her, and yet she couldn't escape the feeling that he was somehow involved in this extremely unpleasant animal export business. Complicating all this was the nagging fear that, incredibly, especially so soon after Mark, she might be starting to fall for him.

Yet he'd refused to catch the bus with her, though he'd known she was desperate to leave Pakburi. He needed to talk to someone at the tiger zoo, he'd said. Could that have been about setting up some kind of deal? If so, Emma couldn't allow that to happen, not after the glimpse of animal suffering she'd already seen. Maybe, if she could ascertain what Dan was up to, she could inform the Thai police of what was about to happen. Whatever, Emma felt confident Dan wouldn't be back for at least another half an hour. She went to Reception. Emma recognised the pretty, young Thai woman behind the desk, who was busy on the phone, looking mildly harassed, clearly trying to placate a difficult customer.

'Help yourself,' she mouthed, indicating

the keys.

'Thank you,' Emma murmured.

On an impulse, Emma reached across, not only for her own key, but also for that of Room 222! Not knowing quite what she was doing, and full of guilt, Emma took the lift up to the second floor and crept stealthily down the corridor till she came to Dan's room. As she unlocked the door, she was wracked by another pang of guilt, but her desperation to know more about Dan overcame the guilt. She pushed the heavy door open.

The room was a mirror image of her own, neat and organised tidily like hers, though naturally more masculine. Not quite sure what she was looking for, other than clues to the real Dan, Emma avoided the bathroom and wardrobe, not wanting to pry into anything more personal than she had to. Instead, she made for the chest of drawers along the wall next to the bed.

On the top of the chest stood Dan's laptop, its lid now firmly closed. There was also a scattering of leaflets on some of Bangkok's animal-based tourist attractions, including the Ancient City and Crocodile Farm, and Thonburi Snake Farm. Turning away with a shudder, Emma slid out the top drawer, finding inside items of stationery, envelopes, Thai postage stamps and headed notepaper. Pulling a sheet of notepaper towards her, Emma frowned at the name and address:

Daniel Fitzgerald, Proprietor, All Creatures Great and Small Zoological Park, Woodhaven, East Sussex.

Emma felt her heart plummet through her body. Dan Fitzgerald owned a zoo? So it seemed he was involved in the animal business, but as for if he was trading in them, of course she didn't know enough of the facts yet to condemn him.

The next drawer contained a number of books on species of animals, and veterinary care. The final drawer held several leaflets and cut-out magazine articles. Flicking through the leaflets and articles with trembling fingers, scanning the words, Emma found to her dismay that they had a recurring theme—buying animals and setting up private zoos.

Suddenly there was the sound of a key in the door. Quickly she jammed the drawer shut, spinning round to face her fate, but to her intense relief, it was a chambermaid who stood in the doorway, not Dan.

'Excuse me,' the maid said apologetically. 'Sorry to disturb you, madam. I've brought fresh towels.'

'Oh—er, thank you,' Emma stammered. 'If you'd just like to take them through to the bathroom. I've got to go out now, anyway. Thank you so much.'

Hurrying back along the corridor, her mind full of tumultuous thoughts, Emma fervently hoped that the chambermaid wouldn't mention the young lady in his room to Dan. At Reception, Emma handed his key back in.

Fortunately, the busy receptionist hung the key back up with scarcely a glance. Emma turned away from the desk, so lost in her thoughts that she literally bumped into Dan himself.

'Emma!' he exclaimed, grasping her shoulders.

Heart pounding, Emma gazed up at him, blushing, full of guilt and confusion. 'Dan,' she replied, as steadily as she could. 'I'd just been to ask if you made it back OK yet.'

The expression in Dan's dark eyes softened as he returned his hands affectionately to her shoulders.

'Thanks, Emma,' he said gently. 'I'm really touched.' Then the corners of this mouth curled. 'But I'm a big boy now. I can look after myself, I promise.'

Emma's embarrassment deepened as she squirmed under his touch, which reminded her uncomfortably of her attraction to him.

'Yes, I know that really. I guess I was just intrigued to see if you'd managed to see the people you wanted to see at the zoo.'

Dan removed his hands from her shoulders. His expression clouded momentarily as if he was mentally distancing himself from her, too.

'Yes. Yes, I did, Emma, thank you.'

On a sudden flash of intuition, Emma

blurted out, 'It was about the girl chimp, wasn't it?'

Dan's eyes widened, as he mouthed, 'Sssh!'

'Did you enquire about buying her?' Emma couldn't help asking.

To her dismay, Dan replied, 'Possibly.'

'Fine, Dan,' she said coolly. 'Don't tell me anything if you don't want to. After all, why change the habit of a lifetime?'

'Emma.' Dan outstretched a hand towards her. 'Don't be like that.' But Emma ignored him.

'I'm flying back to the UK in two days' time, so I don't expect I'll see you again before then. In the meantime, well, it was nice knowing you.'

'Emma!' Dan began, sounding crosser than she had ever heard him, but she stalked off before Dan had a chance to complicate things by making some kind of reply.

As soon as she got round the corner, however, and was waiting for the lift, traitorous tears started to prick her eyes. Resolutely, Emma blinked them away. So, that was the end of her brief personal relationship with Dan Fitzgerald. However, she thought, squaring her shoulders as the lift arrived and she stepped inside, he needn't think she was going to let him off the hook as lightly as that when it came to other matters. Now that she had a suspicion he was possibly setting up a deal to illegally export a wild animal back to Britain. she had a moral obligation to follow up that suspicion.

Leaving the lift, Emma walked down the corridor to her room. She already had a vague idea about what her next move would be. Her ex-boyfriend, Mark, was a reporter on a Brighton-based newspaper, which could pull some useful strings in her investigation of Dan's dealings. Was it wise to phone Mark, though, Emma wondered as she unlocked her door, when she had an inkling that he was still holding some kind of torch for her?

Then Emma thought of the girl chimp at the zoo, and the two baby orang-utans at the market. She banished her fears, flopped down on her bed and pulled the telephone towards her. A minute or so later, the phone at the other end was picked up.

'Mark Frost speaking,' a voice said, sounding surprisingly clear.

'Hello, Mark. It's Emma. Emma Lombard.'

After an unnerving pause on the line, due to the distance between them, Mark replied delightedly, 'Emma! How wonderful to hear from you!'

Resolutely banishing a pang of unease, not to mention a feeling of disloyalty towards Dan, Emma took a deep breath and began to outline to Mark her reasons for calling him.

CHAPTER THREE

Emma sat on the plane, gazing broodingly out of the window. When she'd phoned Mark two days ago, she'd been so caught up in her own concerns that she'd forgotten they were in different time zones. It had been just gone midnight back in the UK, but fortunately Mark had literally been burning the midnight oil, working on an article.

Once he'd got over his initial disappointment that she hadn't called him on personal matters, Mark had taken a keen interest in Emma's tale of Dan Fitzgerald and illegal animal export. They had arranged to meet up and discuss the matter once Emma returned to the UK.

Emma was about to read a magazine when someone said her name. 'Dan,' she said, in some surprise, looking up to see him looming over her. 'Mind if I join you, just for a moment?'

Without waiting for a reply, Dan sat down in the empty seat next to her. Emma shrugged, trying to feign nonchalance while inwardly her heart had started to beat faster.

'If you like. But there's someone sitting there,' she warned, 'and they'll be back in a couple of minutes.'

'No problem. I was hoping I might bump

into you,' Dan said, his dark serious eyes looking right into hers. 'I thought I might see you in the departure lounge but as it turned out, something cropped up and I was running late.'

'You didn't tell me you were flying back the same day as I was,' Emma replied.

'You didn't really give me the chance. But anyway, like you said, Emma, I've only got a couple of minutes so I won't waste time arguing. What I really want to do is what I've been promising you I'd do for ages, and that is explain.'

In spite of herself, Emma's heart leaped in anticipation. Secretly, she longed for Dan to explain and banish every suspicion that she had about him, but she dampened down the eagerness and tried to look nonchalant.

'It's OK, Dan, you don't owe me any explanations,' she said calmly.

'I do,' Dan went on urgently, glancing down the aisle to see if the seats' occupants were returning yet.

Seeing they were not, he turned back to her.

'You see, I know you've probably twigged that I work in some way with animals, but I never got round to explaining to you exactly what I do.' He lowered his voice. 'The fact of the matter is, I own a small private zoo, not far from Brighton, in Woodhaven, to be precise.'

39

'As you may have gathered from our excursions over the past few days, zoos aren't really my kind of thing.'

'Ah, but this isn't any ordinary kind of zoo,' Dan replied. 'You should pop along some time, take a look. Have you got any nephews or nieces?'

'Yes, my sister's got a little boy and girl. Cameron and Annie.'

Dan glanced down the aisle again and Emma followed his gaze.

'Oh, look,' she said in some relief. 'The lady and her son are coming back. I'm sorry, Dan, but it looks like you'd better go.'

Dan turned to Emma with a look of sudden urgency.

'Bring them along to the zoo sometime. Cameron and Annie. Tell them your name at the admissions hut and they'll let you in free of charge.'

Emma managed a smile.

'Thanks. That's a kind offer.'

It was kind, she supposed, but privately, she thought that there was no way she would take children along to a place like Dan Fitzgerald's zoo which was no doubt a den of iniquity and dodgy dealings.

'Keep in touch, Emma,' Dan said casually before he disappeared up the aisle. Emma nodded noncommittally, raising a hand in farewell.

*   *   *

'So, what time are you meeting your ex?'
Alison Stoppard asked in her direct,
straightforward way, as she put the finishing
touches to an eye-catching display.

'I wish you wouldn't call Mark that, Allie. It
sounds—I don't know, as though my only
connection to him is as an old flame.'

'Well, that is your only connection, isn't it?'

'No,' Emma replied indignantly.

Alison, happily engaged herself to Simon,
didn't miss a trick. Emma was thankful she
hadn't mentioned anything about Dan
Fitzgerald to her yet.

'I'd like to think that now, Mark and I are
purely friends. Anyway, to answer your
question, he's calling round here at quarter
past twelve.' Emma looked anxious. 'That is,
presuming it's OK for you to take the late
lunch today.'

'That's fine, honestly, Em.'

Alison smiled back. She ran an efficient
hand through her neat, white-blonde hair. Not
for the first time, Emma felt a pang of
gratitude that Alison was so efficient and
amenable. In fact, Alison, who'd been a
good friend since Emma's schooldays, was
probably one of the reasons why the little
shop had become a moderate success since
Emma had set it up two years ago with a start-
up loan.

41

Mark Frost arrived on the dot of twelve fifteen, as Emma had known he would. He looked immaculately handsome as usual, his fair hair neatly gelled.

'Hi, Emma. You're looking great, like you've caught a bit of sun.'

Mark glanced concernedly at his watch.

'Anyway, enough of the pleasantries. We'd better get a move on, seeing as I'm scheduled for a one-hour lunch, and it would be rather inconvenient to incur the wrath of my editor.'

'No, heaven forbid.'

Emma smiled to herself. In the six months since they'd split up, Mark hadn't changed a bit. She found herself comparing him to Dan. The two men couldn't be more different.

Together, they walked through the overcast March day, down the narrow maze of cobbled lanes, till they came to a small Indian restaurant.

'I thought we'd go for the Indian buffet,' Mark announced, pushing open the door and leading Emma inside.

'Anyway, to get down to business,' Emma announced discreetly across the table once they were settled. 'Like I told you on the phone, Mark, I met this man in Thailand whom I suspect . . .' Feeling an inexplicable flash of disloyalty to Dan, she corrected herself. 'He, it is possible, may be planning to illegally export an endangered animal back to this country.'

Suddenly looking businesslike, as befitted a senior reporter on a top local newspaper, Mark produced a small recorder from his courier bag, pressed a button and set it on the table.

'Now, Emma, would you mind telling me, clearly and carefully, exactly what your grounds are for suspecting this man?'

To the best of her ability, Emma did as Mark asked, telling him about the trips to the animal market and the tiger zoo, what she had found in Dan's hotel room, and finally his admission that he was possibly interested in buying the sick, young chimpanzee.

'I just keep thinking about those dear little baby orang-utans,' Emma finished, her soft eyes welling up with tears. 'And that poor little female chimp with the swollen face.'

'I'm sure it's heartbreaking,' Mark said briskly. 'But we can't afford to be sentimental about this, Emma. That man,' he said, referring to Dan, 'sounds like a rat, and we've got to expose what he's doing at all costs.'

Emma felt another pang of conscience. In spite of everything, she had grown to like Dan.

'What he may be doing, Mark,' she corrected. 'And I'd rather you didn't refer to him as a rat.'

'Why?' Suddenly, Mark looked suspicious. 'There isn't anything personal going on between you and this Fitzgerald bloke, is there?'

'No, not once I realised what he might be up to. It's just that I've got no real proof yet that Dan is going to export a live animal so maybe there isn't really any action we can take.'

Mark dabbed at the corners of his mouth with a napkin.

'Well, I've got an idea, for starters. You and I can visit this zoo of his, have a good snoop round, take advantage of those free tickets he offered you. We'll soon get to the bottom of this. We always did make a good team, Emma.'

From the moment she and Mark arrived at Dan's zoo the following Wednesday, Emma felt jumpy, terrified she'd bump into Dan at any moment.

She didn't know exactly what she had expected to find at Dan's zoo, but whatever it was, she was surprised. The zoo was well laid out, the enclosures of the various animals seemed to be of a good size, and the animals themselves appeared happy and in good condition.

'What do you think of your boss, then?' Mark asked a young, male keeper, as he locked up an enclosure after giving the chimpanzees their food. 'Mr Fitzgerald? What sort of a man is he to work for?'

After looking momentarily bemused, the young man replied, 'What, Dan? Oh, he's a great bloke.' His hazel eyes grew thoughtful.

'Fantastic with the animals, too, and that's what really matters.'

As the young man pushed his trolley on to the next enclosure, Mark switched off the recorder in his pocket and looked disappointed.

'It seems to be the same with everyone we ask,' he muttered. 'Fitzgerald certainly seems to have that lot eating out of his hand.'

'Well, I suppose he can be charming when he puts his mind to it,' Emma admitted, chewing her lip thoughtfully.

'Hmm,' Mark sighed, sounding exasperated. 'His type always is, on the surface. Whatever, we don't seem to be getting anywhere fast. Tell you what, how about you and I split up and do a bit of individual snooping?'

'OK,' Emma agreed, secretly relishing the prospect of a bit of time to herself. Everything seemed above-board at the zoo and she was beginning to wonder if this whole outing was a pointless exercise.

'We could meet up at the café at, say, twelve o'clock?'

'Fine. See you, then.'

As Mark rushed off, recorder in hand, Emma wandered rather aimlessly on to the ring-tailed lemurs' enclosure where the young zoo-keeper was preparing some food on his trolley. He glanced up when he saw Emma, his freckled face breaking into a grin.

'Your boyfriend sure asks a lot of questions, doesn't he?'

'Um, actually, Mark's not my boyfriend,' Emma said quickly, blushing.

'Oh, sorry. Still, your friend knew Dan by name.' His brow creased suddenly. 'Hey, are you from the Inland Revenue or something?'

'No, nothing like that.'

Emma smiled reassuringly to hide her discomfort. She sought for a way of diverting suspicion from herself and took refuge in the truth.

'As a matter of fact, Dan's a sort of friend of mine.' Her blush deepened. 'Actually, we—we met on his recent trip to Thailand.'

'Ah, I see. So Dan's your boyfriend, is that it?'

'No!' Emma replied, her voice almost a squeal. 'Look, anyway,' she said hastily. 'It was nice meeting you, er . . .'

'Tim,' the young man supplied.

'Now I really must go and find my friend, Mark.'

It was only ten to twelve when she got there, so Emma sat at a café table, nursing a cup of coffee while she waited for Mark to arrive. She felt uneasy, unable to shake off the nervous feeling that Dan could appear at any minute. And when Mark strode up to the café, bang on time, his normally amenable features were wearing a thunderous expression.

46

'Asked loads of questions but I didn't get anywhere,' he muttered, flinging himself down in a chair opposite Emma. 'And, to cap it all, I'm starving. I suppose we might as well find out what this place serves in the way of food.'

'Well, I don't know, I'm not really . . .'

At that moment, a cold, familiar voice broke into their conversation.

'Firstly, I'd appreciate it if you would refrain from calling down this award-winning cafeteria, and secondly, I'd be grateful if you, Emma, and especially your friend, would stop distracting my staff from their work by asking pointless questions, the answers to which are none of your business.'

Emma jumped out of her skin. She looked up, straight into Dan Fitzgerald's face! His chocolate eyes were fixed squarely on her, without so much as a glance for Mark. Emma thought she had never seen Dan so angry and she scraped back her chair, squaring her shoulders as she got to her feet.

'You told me to call in sometime, Dan,' she said, trying to sound cool. 'So I simply took you up on your offer.'

Dan glanced scathingly at Mark who was staring at him over the top of the laminated menu with its logo of a cartoon monkey.

'I suggested you might like to bring your nephew and niece,' Dan said shortly. 'I never dreamed that your nephew was the wrong side of thirty.'

Mark, too, got to his feet, his six-foot stature for once dwarfed by Dan's muscular frame.

'I'd appreciate it if you didn't talk to me like that,' he told Dan, eyeing him coldly. 'Your staff all seemed to be deceived by your charm, but underneath it you're really quite a rude man, aren't you?'

'No,' Dan retorted. 'Only to people who've been snooping around my property, prying into my personal affairs. Incidentally, mate, exactly why have you been asking so many questions?'

Instantly, Mark's face took on a sheepish look.

'Come on, Emma. Let's skip lunch, shall we? I think we'd better be going.'

'Hang on a minute.'

Something in Emma rebelled against the proprietorial note in Mark's tone. Thank goodness they'd come in separate cars, she thought, enabling her to retain some measure of independence.

'You leave if you want to, Mark, but I'm not sure I'm . . .'

Mark frowned, his eyes starting to look edgy.

'Come on, Emma. Can't you see there's no pointing staying any longer?'

Suddenly Emma felt a warm, muscular grasp being laid on her wrist which sent a

48

traitorous frisson through her body.

'Emma's not going anywhere just yet,' Dan muttered, glancing at her. 'She and I have got some talking to do first.'

'Fine,' Mark said, shoving in his chair and preparing to leave. 'I'll speak to you later then, Emma.'

With that, he stalked off, jingling his car keys in his hand. When he had gone, any relief Emma might have felt, turned to indignation towards Dan.

'What was with the Neanderthal act just then?' she asked crossly, snatching her wrist away from his grasp.

'Thought we were never going to get rid of your friend there, for a minute,' Dan said, his tone relaxing marginally. 'But I meant what I said just then. You and I do have some serious talking to do. And you can start by telling me what the two of you are doing around here, asking far too many questions for my liking.'

'Questions?' Emma's heart beat faster. 'I suppose your loyal employee, Tim, told tales on us, did he?'

'Tim felt concerned and simply reported back to me like any good member of staff should,' Dan replied, defending the young keeper.

He glanced at his wristwatch then frowned, muttering under his breath.

'I'm expecting an important call in a few minutes and I really need to return to my office to take it in private.'

'An important call?' Emma echoed, her former suspicions of Dan reawakening.

'Anyway, call or no call,' Dan surged on, glancing pointedly at Emma, 'I don't want you doing a disappearing act before we've had a chance to talk.'

'I'm hardly going to allow you to hold me here against my will,' Emma murmured but Dan was ignoring her, his eyes on someone walking past the open-fronted café.

'Kathy,' he called across to the attractive woman who was clad in the navy, zoo staff uniform. 'You couldn't spare me a minute, could you?'

The woman walked over, eyeing first Emma, then returning her gaze to Dan. 'Of course, Dan. I was going to take an early lunch but it's no problem. What can I do for you?'

'Entertain my friend, Miss Lombard, here, for a few moments.'

Dan glanced at his watch again, then meaningfully at Emma.

'Kathy Phillips is my senior zoo-keeper,' he explained. 'You'll be safe in her hands. I'll be back shortly,' and with that he disappeared.

Kathy looked slightly bemused then gestured for Emma to sit back down at the table, doing the same herself.

Oh, well, Emma thought, gazing across at the capable, healthy-looking young woman.

Might as well turn this situation to my advantage.

'So, Kathy,' she began, smiling encouragingly, 'you're the senior zoo-keeper, are you? I suppose that means you must have worked for Dan for some considerable time.'

'Worked with,' Kathy corrected gently. 'Somehow, although Dan's the boss, he always makes one feel as though we're all equals here.'

Kathy's tone was so warm, her green eyes softening so at the mention of Dan's name, that Emma couldn't help wondering about the relationship between the two of them.

'It's safe to say that the two of you get on well, then?' Emma asked.

'Yes, very well,' Kathy replied, and Emma was surprised to feel a pang of jealousy as Kathy continued politely, 'so, Miss Lombard . . .'

'Call me Emma,' Emma urged, instinctively liking the woman in spite of everything.

'Emma, how do you know Dan?'

Emma was just finishing giving an edited version of her encounters with Dan in Thailand, in which Kathy seemed very interested, when the man himself reappeared. He rubbed his large hands together in a satisfied way.

'Right, that's that taken care of. Thanks very much for your services, Kathy. You go and have your lunch now, before you expire

51

from hunger.'

With one last, curious glance at Emma and Dan, Kathy rose from her chair and disappeared.

'We can't talk here,' Dan said, gesturing at the busy café. 'Shall we go for a walk? There's something I need to tell you and it requires a bit of privacy.'

Intrigued, Emma got to her feet, smoothing down the pale linen trousers. Together they left the café and walked off down one of the zoo's winding, leafy avenues. They walked close together and Dan's voice was low and confidential.

'You see,' he explained, as they strolled, 'I've only told you part of the story regarding what I do, vocation-wise.' He looked across at her. 'And I gather from the activities of you and your friend this morning, that you've still got certain suspicions about me which need to be laid to rest.'

Emma opened her mouth to deny this then realised it would be pointless and closed it again.

'Firstly,' Dan went on, gesturing about him, 'this isn't a zoo as such, more of an animal sanctuary, meaning that we give homes to animals rescued from dangerous and cruel situations around the globe.'

Emma gave a low gasp of realisation.

'A sanctuary? I see.'

But the facts still didn't add up. How could

she just dismiss her suspicions about Dan and endangered animals?

'And the second thing, the second half of what I do, is that I work undercover, investigating the illegal animal trade.'

CHAPTER FOUR

Two hours later, Dan had left the closing of the zoo in Kathy's capable hands, and he and Emma were driving separately to a nearby country pub, Dan's local. Dan was greeted warmly by the barman.

'I know it's a bit early for a drink,' Dan said wryly, as they sat down at a secluded corner table, 'but it's non-alcoholic, and we need a quiet place to talk.'

'Cheers, anyway,' Emma said ironically, as she raised her glass of pineapple juice, and Dan raised his pint of orange juice and lemonade. 'So,' she began, in a low voice. 'You were investigating the illegal animal trade in Thailand. Where exactly did I fit into the picture, Dan?'

'You were so keen to come to the animal market with me that first day,' he said, 'so in the end I caved in, thinking it might be useful to gain an impartial viewpoint.'

'So you were using me!'

'Maybe you and I were using each other,' Dan suggested mildly. 'After all, you were insistent on coming to that animal market with me.'

'Maybe,' Emma conceded reluctantly, and she sensed it was time for a confession of her own. 'And my own behaviour hasn't exactly been above reproach. I sneaked into your hotel room for a snoop around, the afternoon we went to the tiger zoo.'

Emma tensed, waiting for Dan's thunderous outburst, but it did not come. 'Ah, so it was you,' he said, raising his eyebrows. 'I had my suspicions.'

'You did?' Emma asked tentatively.

Dan nodded.

'I could tell some of my stuff had been moved around. I'm a very particular person,' he added sternly, in a voice that made her quail inside. 'But nothing had been taken. Then, when the chambermaid mentioned my young lady friend the next morning, I put two and two together.'

Emma coloured deeply.

'And there I was, passing judgement on you. It turns out that I'm the one who behaved abominably, while you're the one who spends his time jetting around the world, saving animals left, right and centre.'

Dan shrugged his broad shoulders.

'Let's call it quits, shall we? I'm no saint, as you know, Emma. I'm a qualified vet, but it was always my dream to set up a refuge for mistreated or endangered animals. It's just that, now my animal sanctuary is well established and profitable, I've got sufficient time and money to pursue my conservational interests.'

He paused to take a long draught of

his drink.

'I have contacts in a local Thai animal welfare group. I work in conjunction with some of its members and these were some of my business appointments while I was over there. Also,' Dan admitted, 'I was filming my investigations while I was in Bangkok.'

Emma's chestnut-brown eyes widened.

'But how . . .' She stopped. 'The black courier bag that went everywhere with you!' she said slowly, in realisation. 'That had your camcorder in it, didn't it?' Dan nodded, confirming her thoughts.

'Guilty as charged. Bit risky, I guess. Mind you, I got some extremely useful footage out of it.'

'So, where else have your investigations taken you?' Emma asked, intrigued.

'All over,' Dan replied nonchalantly. 'I've investigated the welfare of cheetahs in South Africa, tigers in India, orang-utans in Jakarta . . .'

With a pang, Emma remembered those baby orang-utans in Bangkok.

'In south-east Asia,' Dan went on, breaking the moment, 'thousands of endangered animals are stolen from the wild every day. The illegal animal trade is worth billions of pounds.'

'No wonder you feel so strongly about it,' Emma commented. 'At first, out in Thailand, I thought you seemed so calm about the horrors of it all.'

'I've seen so much. I'm almost numb to it now. Part of the problem in Thailand is that there's a law that states that if an animal is already in the country, it can be bred from. Also, if an animal was bred in captivity, it's legal to sell it. Poachers often lie that an animal was bred in captivity.'

'So how do you tell the difference between an animal bred in captivity, and one stolen from the wild?' Emma asked.

'An animal from the wild is naturally scared of humans, whereas one reared in captivity is used to people, and that shows in the way they respond to them.'

'So, what's happening now with your investigations?'

'The conference, called to discuss the illegal animal trade, has put paid to my investigations for the time being, particularly concerning those two baby orang-utans.'

'You didn't want to buy those two orang-utans for yourself at all!' Emma exclaimed in sudden realisation. 'You just wanted to expose the dealers by setting up a fake deal.'

'And then call in the police,' Dan agreed. 'My cover story to dealers is that I want to set up my own small zoo in the UK. I don't want them to think I'm particularly expert in this field, though. However, in any case, our friend, Lek, at the animal market, will be feeling far too shifty to conduct a deal with me at the moment.'

'That's a shame,' Emma said feelingly.

'I don't know about you,' Dan said suddenly, 'but all this talking has given me an appetite. I'm starving.' He got to his feet. 'I'm going to order us some sandwiches. Don't run away now, will you?'

Later, while they ate the sandwiches, Emma began tentatively, 'So, now I've forgiven you for using me in your investigation, Dan, have you forgiven me for snooping round your zoo today?'

'Should I forgive you,' he asked, his dark eyes boring directly into Emma's, 'or your friend?'

'I'd better explain what we were doing,' she said. 'You see, Mark is a senior reporter. When I thought you might be involved with the illegal animal trade, Dan, I rang Mark up, wondering if he would be interested in writing an article. He said he was.' Emma paused. 'Now I know you're on the level, I suppose there's no reason why Mark shouldn't go ahead and write the article anyway.'

For the first time during this exchange, a thunderous expression passed across Dan's face.

'On the contrary,' he said. 'An article at this stage would be extremely counter-productive! It could expose my cover, for starters.'

Emma looked anxious.

'Of course! I hadn't thought of that. I'd

better halt Mark.'

'You do that.' Dan raised a dark eyebrow. 'So, see a lot of this Mark?'

'I might ask the same of you and Kathy Phillips,' Emma countered. 'She spoke very warmly of you.'

'Kathy's a good woman, but we're just colleagues,' Dan said.

'Well, Mark and I used to go out together,' Emma explained, relieved. 'But we're just friends now.'

Emma didn't know if she imagined it, but Dan almost permitted himself a smile at this. Emma smiled back, and felt the familiar spark of attraction ignite between them. Dan cleared his throat.

'Good grief! We've been talking for hours. It's after six. How about one proper drink, before we go our separate ways?'

'OK,' Emma conceded with a grin, 'but I'd better make it half a shandy, if I want to retain full control of my faculties.'

As they relaxed over their drinks, Emma began to think again what a likeable man Dan was.

'It's a shame about Mark's article,' she mused, after a while, as they finished their drinks and wandered out into the cooling evening air. 'He's a competent journalist and I'm sure it would have been a good piece. I hope he won't be too disappointed.'

'He'll get over it, I'm sure.'

They walked towards their cars in the pub car park. As they stopped walking, he suddenly took Emma in his arms, and kissed her.

*　　　*　　　*

A week later, Emma was still dazed and confused in the wake of that kiss. Of course, it had been passionate, and at the time she had enjoyed it greatly, believing the feeling had been mutual, that their personal relationship may be back on. So why, she wondered unhappily, had a week passed with not a word from Dan. She had tried to keep herself busy and distracted, paying visits to her mother, father and sister, but in vain.

It was Wednesday again, and Emma and Alison were working in the shop, when the phone went. Alison answered it.

'Good morning, how can I help you?' Her polite, smiling expression dropped. 'Oh, yes. I'll get her for you. It's your ex,' Alison mouthed, pulling a face.

Emma gave her friend a mock scowl, walking over to the back of the shop and taking the cordless phone from her.

'Thanks. Hello, Mark,' she into the mouthpiece.

'Hi, there, Em. It's good to hear your voice,' Mark said warmly and Emma squirmed uncomfortably. 'I just wanted to ask you something about the article.'

'Mark!' Emma exclaimed reprovingly. 'I thought I told you the article had to be put on hold indefinitely, or you'll blow Dan's cover.'

'Hmm, if you believe Fitzgerald's story, and he really is innocent in all this,' Mark muttered. 'Anyway, I don't see any harm in my preparing the article in the meantime, so that it's ready to go to press as soon as the situation allows.'

'This is a serious situation, Mark,' Emma said in a low voice. 'Dan says there are animal racketeers out there who've threatened to kill people who get involved. If anything goes wrong, Dan's life could be put in danger.'

Looking up, Emma almost jumped out of her skin, for Dan himself was standing in front of her, watching her intently.

'Look, Mark, I've got to go. We'll talk later, but, please, think seriously about what I've said.'

She switched the phone off, and for a moment, Dan just stared at her, smiling almost imperceptibly. The attraction crackled between them.

Then Dan said quietly, 'I couldn't help overhearing just then. You seemed to be expressing concern for my wellbeing.'

Emma flushed. She said coolly, 'Don't worry about Mark. I'll make sure he doesn't publish the article before you're ready.'

'I'm not worried about Mark,' Dan said in a

low, meaningful voice. 'Not at this precise moment.'

The atmosphere between them was becoming more charged by the second. Emma glanced around the shop, but thankfully Alison was busy attending to a customer.

'Look, Emma,' Dan went on, 'I'm sorry I haven't got in touch before, but the past week's been really hectic.'

'Yes, I can imagine. You're a very popular man,' Emma said, her hurt making her sarcastic.

Dan's mouth twisted.

'I just wanted to say how much I enjoyed our evening together last week.'

'Me, too,' Emma had to admit, her voice coming out a little croaky.

The shop bell jangled as the customer left the shop with her purchase. Alison gave Emma and Dan a swift, curious glance, then turned away discreetly. Dan moved closer to Emma, taking one of her hands in his.

'Anyway, I wanted to let you know that I'm going to be rather busy over the next couple of days, but I'll be in touch.'

'I see,' Emma said, her heart pounding.

Dan leaned forward, to kiss her gently on the lips. The kiss made Emma melt, and she found herself forgiving Dan everything.

'Look, I've got to go.' He looked regretful. 'But take care, won't you?'

'Yes. You, too,' Emma added, feeling

slightly bemused as Dan released her hand.

He smiled a goodbye at Alison and left the shop. Emma was left, feeling unsure as to exactly what Dan's visit had meant. Alison widened her grey-blue eyes behind their glasses.

'Wow! You dark horse, Emma! Where have you been hiding him? If I wasn't a happily engaged woman I'd snap him up. He's gorgeous!'

When Emma told her all about Dan, about his zoo, though not about his undercover investigations, Alison was insistent that she should make the next move. Emma wondered if her friend was right.

Two days later, egged on by Alison, Emma went up to her flat above the shop, in her lunch hour. She rang the zoo and asked for Dan Fitzgerald. 'Who's calling, please?' the female voice at the other end asked.

'Emma Lombard.' Emma paused, then asked hesitantly, 'That isn't Kathy by any chance, is it?'

'It is. Hi, Emma!' Kathy hesitated. 'I'm afraid Dan's going to be away from the zoo for a few days,' she continued, in her kind, no-nonsense voice. 'In fact, he couldn't say exactly how long he would be off for.'

Emma almost quit, but thought of Alison, and steeled herself.

'In that case, you couldn't possibly give me his home number, could you, Kathy? Only it's quite important that I get in touch with him.'

There was another brief hesitation.

'I could give you Dan's home number, sure,' Kathy replied, sounding uncertain as to how much she should say. 'But the thing is, he's actually out of the country at the moment.'

'He's gone back to Bangkok, hasn't he?' Emma burst out.

It seemed Kathy, too, was forced into honesty.

'Oh, Emma, he has. He would have told you, but . . .'

'It's OK, Kathy,' Emma interrupted. 'Don't you worry about it. It's not your fault. Thanks for all your help anyway. Goodbye.'

As she put the phone down, tears seeped into Emma's eyes. She felt desperate to confide in someone, and wandered back down to the shop. Fortunately, Alison was alone.

'You've been crying, haven't you?' Allie asked, concerned, handing her a tissue. 'Come on, out with it.'

Emma explained that Dan had gone away, though not about his undercover mission.

'I just feel hurt and cross that he's gone away to Bangkok without telling me and worse still, that he confided in this attractive female colleague of his.'

Every time she thought she was getting to know him, he let her down again, unwilling to take her into his confidence. Alison's response was rousing. 'Where's your backbone, woman? You've got to go after the divine Daniel yourself, even if it means following him to Thailand.'

Suddenly, Emma knew that Alison was right. She felt a personal involvement in this investigation, there was no denying it, and she was damned if Dan was going to deny her the opportunity to witness its outcome!

'You're right, Allie,' she said. 'I'm going to go back upstairs and try to book a flight right now.'

She would close the shop temporarily if she had to, but she was going to give Dan Fitzgerald the biggest surprise of his life, and join him in Thailand. Back upstairs, Emma lifted the phone again, pulled the Yellow Pages towards her, and began to ring round the travel agents, enquiring about the soonest available flights to Bangkok.

*   *   *

'You may now unfasten your seatbelts,' the voice said over the loudspeaker in the plane after take-off.

Emma unfastened her seatbelt, feeling as if she was in a daze. Everything seemed to have happened in a rush. She had impulsively booked her flight to Bangkok, had phoned her family to let them know she'd be out of the country again, and then phoned Mark to update him on the situation.

'Are you sure this is wise?' Mark had asked, sounding concerned after grilling Emma on her plans, including the airline and time of her flight.

'Of course,' Emma replied promptly, banishing her inner qualms. 'You know me. I'm not normally an impulsive person. But this time, inside, I just feel sure I'm doing the right thing.'

'You take care, though. I'm not one hundred per cent certain that Fitzgerald is on the level.'

'Of course he is, I know that now!'

And now, here she was, on the plane, heading off halfway round the world to Bangkok on some mad whim. Settling herself down for the long, non-stop flight, Emma was stunned to hear a voice say her name. Her first thought was of Dan but, glancing up, she stared right into Mark's face. There he stood in the aisle, next to her seat. Emma did a double-take.

'Bet this is a surprise.' Mark grinned sheepishly at her. 'Only just made it on to the flight, as a matter of fact, something that's never happened to me before. Booking this whole thing up was rather a last-minute affair.'

'But what are you doing here?' Emma stuttered in amazement.

'This has the makings of a huge article, Emma. It could earn me a long-overdue promotion. Besides, I thought I'd better come to keep an eye on you.'

'As a friend, I hope, Mark, just as a friend, the same way I think of you.'

Emma and Mark checked into separate rooms at the Indira Hotel, with Emma reluctantly agreeing to meet Mark later for dinner. Still, she had felt her spirits lift from the moment she had arrived back in Bangkok. By late afternoon, she had unpacked, showered and changed into a cool, cotton sarong and top, swept up her hair, and gone down to Reception to enquire as to the room number of a Mr Daniel Fitzgerald.

Minutes later, she was knocking on his door, praying that he would be in. He was, apparently. She heard noises from within, and his voice, sounding mildly impatient, saying, 'Coming.'

Her heart lurched as the door was flung open and Dan's broad-shouldered figure filled the doorway. For a moment, he just stared at her, as if unable to believe what he saw. The tension crackled between them. Emma met his gaze, lifting her chin with a hint of defiance.

'Hello, Dan,' she managed to say, trying to sound as smooth as possible.

She tried to make a joke out of it but was surprised to hear how husky her voice sounded.

'You just can't get rid of me, can you?'

CHAPTER FIVE

Dan's eyes darkened as he stared at Emma in devious astonishment. 'What the heck are you doing here, Emma?' he said eventually.

'Aren't you going to ask me in, Dan, so that I can explain?'

'Of course. Come on in, then.'

Dan offered Emma the chair from the desk, then plonked himself down on the bed opposite her.

After a moment's charged silence, he said, 'Come on then, Emma, tell me what you're doing here.' His brows furrowed. 'And this had better be good.'

'I could equally well ask you why you came back to Bangkok without telling me where you were going, or giving me the opportunity to join you,' she replied, looking Dan straight in the eye. 'I noticed, however, that you did choose to confide in your rather attractive senior zoo-keeper, Kathy.'

'There's no need to say it in that tone, Emma. I confided in Kathy because we're work colleagues, and this investigation is inextricably linked with my business.' He sighed. 'I've told you before that there's nothing personal between Kathy and me.'

'Oh,' Emma said, slightly mollified. 'All right, if you insist. But don't dodge the main issue, Dan,' she went on, rallying once again. 'You still didn't tell me you were sneaking off to Thailand!'

'I didn't tell you where I was going precisely because I knew you would want to come with me! And this situation is too dangerous for you to get involved with, Emma.'

'Why?' she asked indignantly. 'Because I'm a woman?'

'Call me old-fashioned but, yes, partly.' Dan's voice grew softer, more kind. 'But also because you're inexperienced, and this investigation, in all honesty, is none of your concern.'

'But I felt, after we spent all that time together out here before, visiting the animal market and the zoo, that the two of us were in on this together.' Her chestnut eyes sparked sudden fire. 'And you were happy enough to use me when it suited you, to make you appear more like a naïve tourist by having a particularly naïve friend in tow!'

'Come on, we've been over all this before.'

'I know,' Emma said exasperatedly. 'And I can tell you don't want to rake over it all again.'

She got to her feet, scraping back the chair.

'I can also tell when I'm not wanted. So I'm going now.'

Dan, too, got to his feet, grabbing her hand as she moved to leave. 'It's not that you're not wanted, Emma. You know that.'

69

Instantly, the mood altered. The touch of his hand did something to Emma, calming her. Dan pulled her to him, encircling his other arm around the small of her back.

'Well, you didn't seem exactly delighted to see me, just now,' Emma murmured.

'Didn't I?'

Slowly, Dan bent his head to hers and kissed her. They finally pulled apart and Dan said huskily, 'Let's just say that I'm starting to come round to the idea of you being here.'

'So,' Emma began, clearing her throat, 'aren't you going to update me on how the investigation's going?'

'I haven't made too much headway, especially seeing as I myself only arrived here yesterday. I had a brief business meeting this morning but we'll have to wait and see how that pans out.' He paused. 'My main plan for now it to return to Pakburi Tiger Zoo tomorrow, to check up on the young female chimp with the mouth abscess. Cori, that was her name.'

'So you were only interested in that little chimp because you were concerned about her health?' she asked.

Dan nodded, his mouth a straight, uncompromising line.

'I'll bet it's easy to get emotionally involved.'

Dan grunted his agreement.

'So, anyway, I gave the trainer some advice

on antibiotics and nutrition last time I was here. If I—we—go back tomorrow and the creature's doing OK, I'll be content for her to stay in Bangkok, certainly for now, anyway. If, however, her condition has deteriorated, I may have to take drastic measures.'

'Oh, so you don't mind me going along with you tomorrow?' Emma asked tentatively, trying to hide her keenness.

She desperately wanted to see little Cori for herself, to banish that feeling that something terrible had happened to her. Dan looked her straight in the eye, in a way that made her momentarily forget her concerns.

'No, Emma, as long as you're discreet, and take care, I might as well resign myself to the fact that you're coming along with me.'

Emma leaned forward to give Dan a playful whack on the arm.

'You could sound a bit more keen than that!'

The atmosphere certainly seemed to be thawing between them. Then suddenly Emma remembered something that put the brakes on her rising spirits. 'There's something else I should tell you.'

'What's that?'

'I'm not here on my own. You see, the thing is, Mark Frost is here, too.'

'What's he doing here?' Dan exploded. 'Have I missed the point? Is this some cosy little break for two?'

71

'Of course not!' Emma retorted indignantly. 'I told you, Mark and I are just friends now.'

'So what is Frost doing here,' Dan reiterated, calming slightly, 'if there's nothing in it for him, romantically speaking?'

'Mark is first and foremost a journalist, and a good one at that,' she replied. 'He's obsessed with this being such a hot story. And he's got a point. It could help your cause, to have a journalist in on the investigation.'

'As long as he doesn't publish the article before we've got things tied up here! Otherwise I'll be sorely tempted to break every bone in his body.'

'No, I swear Mark won't jeopardise things for you,' Emma promised. Sensing that Dan's mood had now worsened, Emma got to her feet. 'Well, anyway, I think I'd better be going.'

Dan rose, too, his earlier warmth and passion now replaced by cool formality.

'I think it'd be just as well if you did. I've got plenty of business to catch up on, and the two of you needn't worry about bumping into me in the restaurant tonight. I think I'll call room service, so that I can keep working.'

As Emma opened the door, Dan added gruffly, 'I'm not happy about Frost being over here, but as he's here I suppose you might as well tell him he can come along to the zoo with us tomorrow morning.'

'Thank you,' Emma said, with genuine gratitude.

She looked into Dan's eyes, hoping to see there an echo of some of his former warmth and tenderness towards her, but all she saw was cold blankness, and hurt. In response, she felt an answering pain in her own heart, like a knife twisting. With a start, she realised that her feelings for Dan had started to grow into something more than simple attraction.

*   *   *

The final ripples of applause faded from around the circus ring, and spectators began to gather bags and coats together, and prepare to leave the arena. Emma, however, was not clapping. For one thing, she had not particularly enjoyed the show, and for another, she was feeling too apprehensive about what was to come.

'Disgusting,' Mark commented loudly, from where he sat to her right. Throughout the performance, he had been alternately jotting down notes in his pad and snapping away with his zoom lens camera.

'That sort of thing shouldn't be allowed in this day and age.'

'Come on, Mark,' Emma said placatingly. 'We didn't come here to enjoy the show. We came here to do a job, remember.'

From Emma's other side, Dan grunted.

'Emma's right,' he said, leaning forward to address Mark. 'And if you continue to make loud remarks of an uncomplimentary nature, Frost, we aren't going to be very welcome here. That'll stop us from carrying out the important task we've come to do.'

Not for the first time that day, Emma felt like piggy in the middle, caught between the two men who were barely tolerating each other. At best, one could say that an uneasy truce existed between them.

'Yes, boss,' Mark said, with a heavy irony, getting to his feet. 'Now come on, let's get this show on the road.'

Emma and Dan stood, too, and the unlikely threesome made their way down to the front of the arena.

'I'm not sure if I could see little Cori during the show,' Emma murmured anxiously as they walked. 'I mean, I saw a chimp in a yellow cardigan and tutu, like she was wearing before, but I couldn't be sure if that was her or her replacement. I hope she's OK.'

'I'm pretty sure that was her,' Dan muttered back. 'But we were sitting too far away to distinguish any swelling on her face.'

Dan approached one of the trainers who was clearing up.

'Excuse me, it's Juan, isn't it? Dan Fitzgerald. I'm a qualified vet. I spoke to you a few weeks ago regarding one of your young female chimpanzees, Cori,' he explained.

74

Juan's face broke into a smile of recognition.

'Ah, Dan,' he said, extending his hand for the other man to shake. 'Yes, I remember. Good to see you again. I'll go and fetch Cori,' he added.

As soon as Juan reappeared, with the young chimp in his arms, Emma could see that she was greatly recovered.

'The swelling has gone completely!' she murmured, unable to stop herself. 'Oh, sweetheart, you look so much better,' she said in relief.

Dan cleared his throat impatiently.

'When you're ready, Emma,' he said drily, but with a touch of humour, 'if you wouldn't mind letting the qualified vet have a look. Yes, the swelling does seem to have cleared up completely,' he said. 'Excellent.'

A smile broke over his face like sun emerging from clouds, and even his bluff manner was unable to disguise his pleasure. Juan, too, seemed pleased.

'We've been following your advice on nutrition and antibiotics,' he said, 'not just with Cori, but with the other animals, too. We can't thank you enough for your help, Mr Fitzgerald.'

'Well, at least that's one story with a happy ending,' Emma said, as she, Dan and Mark left the zoo and went to wait for a bus back to the hotel.

'Now, now, Emma, I'm sure you're aware that it's not a simple happy ever after,' Dan corrected her with a wry smile, as they arrived at the bus stop. 'I shall be checking up on Cori's progress from time to time, make no mistake about that.'

Emma nodded. 'It was hard saying goodbye to that little creature, knowing I might never see her again,' she admitted, her eyes filling with moisture. 'I was almost hoping that you were going to have to bring her back to Britain, Dan.'

'Yes, well just be thankful that that won't be necessary.'

There was a loud grunt from nearby, reminding them of Mark's presence.

'I don't know where your happy ending leaves my article, either, Emma,' he said moodily.

Ever since they had met up with Juan, Mark had seemed dejected and sullen, almost resentful that things had turned out OK for Cori.

'It's hardly going to make a dramatic scoop, the case of an animal being well-treated.'

A bus rumbled up to the stop, and Mark swept bad-temperedly ahead of Emma and Dan. Left together, they exchanged glances. At that moment, Dan's mobile phone trilled. He reached for it.

'Hello? Ah, yes, hello,' he said, sounding eager. 'Tonight. Great. I'll be there.''

Dan switched off the phone, and he and Emma joined the end of the queue.

'That was Lek, the dealer from the animal market,' he said, close to Emma's ear. 'In the rush yesterday I didn't tell you. I met up briefly with Lek and his friend, Gharma, yesterday morning. I met up with those two baby orang-utans again, too.'

'You didn't!' Emma gasped.

Dan nodded. 'The deal — should I say the fake deal—with the baby orang-utans could be back on. I'm meeting up with the men again tonight.'

'Hold on a minute,' Emma corrected, looking into his eyes as they boarded the bus, and feeling a rush of nervous excitement. 'Don't you mean we're meeting up with them tonight?'

Dan glanced across at her. A smile twitched the corners of his mouth.

'You never give up, do you, Emma? Very well, come with me if you wish. Lek might recognise you from before and that could count in our favour. But we've got to keep this low-key, so I'm afraid we'll have to leave your friend Mark out of this one.'

'Don't worry, I'll take care of him,' Emma promised as they entered the crowded stuffiness of the bus and looked about for Mark.

She wondered exactly how she was going to shake Mark off later, but that was the least of her worries. Most pressing of all was a sudden surge of foreboding about the safety of tonight's rendezvous, and what dangers might be awaiting both her and Dan.

'You take the seat next to Mark,' Dan told Emma as they made their way down the bus. 'I'll take the one behind.'

'OK,' Emma murmured in reply.

It wasn't the most comfortable of journeys, as far as Dan was concerned. He was confronted by the view of Emma's chestnut brown head next to Mark's blond one. They were conversing in a desultory way about something or other, but Dan had no desire to eavesdrop. He was unsure what the relationship between those two was, and didn't particularly feel like probing his feelings to see if he cared either way.

Maybe Emma herself wasn't sure about the nature of her feelings for Mark Frost. Dan sighed heavily as the bus bumped along, and he turned his head towards the window to his right. What was it to him, anyway? He tried unsuccessfully to concentrate on the glimpses of emerald palm trees between the bobbing heads of the passengers, and block out everything else.

Back in her hotel room that afternoon, Emma felt both nervous and excited, and the hours until evening stretched ahead of her. She felt a sudden need to hear the voice of a good friend and, checking her watch, she calculated what the time would be in Britain right now. Reaching for her mobile phone, she keyed in the code for the UK, followed by Alison's home number. It rang a few times before Alison's voice answered.

'Oh, Allie, it's me,' Emma said in grateful relief. 'How's things?'

'Em! Great to hear from you,' Alison replied. 'Simon and I were just about to settle down to watch a video. It's been pretty hectic this end. You know what Sundays are like in the shop.'

'That's fantastic, Allie. I can't tell you how grateful I am for you taking over the reins at such short notice.'

'No probs. So how are things going with you, then?' Alison asked. 'How's your exotic break? Have you made a move on the gorgeous Dan yet?'

Emma sighed deeply. Suddenly, the need to unburden herself to an old friend pressed upon her harder than ever. Also, she felt guilty at keeping the truth about her trip from her friend, when Alison had been so good to her.

'Why the sigh?' Alison asked in the face of Emma's continuing silence. 'Do I take it that things aren't going too well on that front?' She sounded genuinely astonished. 'Surely he hasn't rejected your advances.'

'Let's just say,' she began slowly, 'that, though I like Dan, and I think he likes me,

Dan and I have had other things on our minds, besides romance. For starters, Mark has turned up over here as well, and you could say that three's a crowd.'

Now Alison sounded flabbergasted.

'Mark Frost? Your ex? What the heck's he doing over there?'

Carefully, Emma explained the situation to Alison, from start to finish, about Dan's investigation of the animal export trade, and Mark's desire to write an article on it.

'I feel so bad about keeping all this from you for so long,' Emma finished, 'but Dan stressed that people's lives could be at risk if a word of all this got out.' She drew a shaky breath. 'Only I've got to the stage where, if I didn't talk to a good friend soon, I felt I'd burst.'

'Oh, Emma, of course I don't mind you not telling me,' Alison said earnestly. 'But if you had, I'd have told you to take care, which I'm going to say to you now, anyway. The shop needs you back in one piece. I need you back in one piece. Take care, please.'

'I will, but I just want to tell you that this is important to me. I wouldn't have temporarily abandoned the business, if it wasn't.'

'OK, I hear what you're saying, but this fake deal business sounds pretty risky to me, pulling the wool over the eyes of those dealers. They could be dangerous men.'

'Oh, Alison.' Emma's voice beseeched her

friend to understand. 'I've met one of them already. He seems just like you and me.'

'Appearances can be deceptive, though. Take care.'

*   *   *

'I feel like a child bunking off school,' Emma confessed to Dan as they whizzed along in the taxi that night, strings of diamond lights snaking past them in the darkness. 'A mixture of nervousness and guilt.'

It was true. Butterflies of apprehension were dancing in her stomach. His craggy face illuminated intermittently by the passing street lamps, Dan grinned back at her.

'So, how did you shake off our friend Mr Frost in the end?'

'We met for dinner in the hotel restaurant at seven, as usual. Then I told him I was tired, and wanted to go straight to my room afterwards for an early night.'

'He was probably hoping for a full evening of your undivided attention, as he received last night.'

'Oh, no,' she said feeling indignant. 'Don't get hold of the wrong end of the stick, Dan. No doubt you're imagining that Mark and I spent yesterday evening together, lingering cosily over dinner, sharing a few drinks in the bar afterwards, getting romantic over the brandies. In fact, you're probably imagining that Mark and I spent the time rekindling our old relationship!'

'Now, now,' Dan said quickly, holding up a defensive hand. 'I never said anything of the sort.'

'No, but I'm sure you're thinking it,' Emma replied, her feelings betrayed by her rising colour. 'Whereas, in reality, all that Mark and I shared last night was a single after-dinner coffee in the hotel bar before going our separate ways!'

'So Mark wasn't disappointed tonight, then?' Dan asked.

'Mark was fine about it, really,' Emma said.

'You seem to care a lot about Frost's feelings,' Dan grunted.

Emma was wondering how to respond to this when the taxi pulled up outside a bar on the far side of Bangkok.

'Well, this is it,' Dan announced.

Glancing at the neon-lit, bustling premises, in the busy street, Emma felt another twinge of foreboding.

'I hope you know what you're doing, Dan Fitzgerald,' she muttered. 'Don't worry, I'll take care of you,' Dan replied in a low voice.

Emma glanced at the bulk of Dan, on the seat next to her, and found something reassuring in his broad, muscled arms.

'I might hold you to that.'

Dan grinned at her, and she grinned back. Then he paid the driver and they got out.

Inside the bar, Dan spied the two men he was looking for immediately. 'Lek, Gharma,' he greeted them, leading Emma to the corner table where both men sat looking wary. Emma felt her stomach turn over with nerves. The men each had a bottled lager on the table in front of them.

'Hello, again, Dave,' they greeted him—so Dan had given himself an alias. The pair rose to shake Dan's hand, then Emma's.

'My friend, Elizabeth,' Dan explained to the men.

Emma was a little taken aback that she, too, had a new name and flashed Dan a glance.

'Ah, yes, Elizabeth,' the shorter of the two men said, whom Emma recognised as Lek. 'I remember her, from the market.'

'Hello again, Lek,' Emma murmured. 'Pleased to meet you, Gharma.'

All four of them sat down. Dan hailed a waiter and ordered more bottled lagers all round. After taking a swig of his lager, Dan got straight down to business. Fortunately, there was no chance of them being overheard, amidst the din of the bar.

'So, the deal's still on, I take it?'

Lek's dark eyes flicked towards Gharma and then back at Dan. He answered in a low voice.

'Yes, but we need the money up front.'

Gharma added for clarification, 'You give us the money for each orang-utan tonight.'

'Tonight?' Dan raised his eyebrows. 'When do we get the animals?'

'Tomorrow, as soon as you can finalise the details,' Lek replied.

Dan frowned, stroking his jaw.

'I see.'

Emma realised he was playing a part, that of the hard bargainer. Dan glanced at her, as if to question the decision with her. Playing along with it, she nodded, then Dan turned back to the men. He sighed, as if in capitulation.

'OK. Tonight I give you the agreed sum,' he said.

'All right. You pay us in English pounds, of course?' Lek said in reply.

'Of course.'

'Agreed.'

'How will I get the creatures out of the country safely?' Dan asked.

Now it was Gharma's turn to speak.

'We have contacts at the airport,' he said. 'They will make sure your orang-utans get through Customs as luggage.'

This seemed incredible to Emma. Setting down her glass, she frowned.

'Luggage? How on earth will you disguise them as luggage?' she asked.

'Simple, Elizabeth,' Gharma said, his fingers encircling the neck of his lager bottle. 'The animals will be placed in two boxes in a bag.'

'Enough talking,' Lek interrupted, looking edgy. 'You have the money?'

'Yes, yes, don't worry.'

Dan smiled in a reassuring way. Reaching into his pocket, he withdrew his wallet. Then, under the table, he carefully counted two thousand pounds in fifty pound notes. Emma's eyes were like saucers at the amount of cash changing hands, wondering where Dan had obtained it from.

Lek took the money, then re-counted it. Finally he pocketed the notes, looking very serious.

'Shall we shake on it?' Dan asked and shook hands with each of the men.

'Tomorrow,' Lek said. 'You are ready to carry out the deal tomorrow?'

Again Dan glanced questioningly at Emma.

'Tomorrow's fine,' she replied.

'We'll book ourselves on to the first available flight,' Dan continued.

Lek downed the last of his beer.

'You two will go to the airport, to the appropriate gate for your flight. We will sort that tomorrow. You can let me know the details. Then Gharma will deal with the man at the X-ray machine to let you through.'

'OK,' Dan and Emma said together.

'When do we get the animals?' Dan asked.

'When you know the details of your flights, you come to our yard, to receive the animals. If necessary, we travel to the airport together,'

Gharma continued.

'Together?' Emma queried, surprised.

'Together, if need be,' Gharma confirmed. 'We take no chances. The address of the yard is 21, Orchid Road.'

'Till tomorrow, then,' Dan said.

'Tomorrow,' Lek echoed hastily, before the two men disappeared into the crowds in the bar, then out into the night, just visible through the open doorway.

When they had gone, Emma breathed a shaky sigh, half of relief, half of renewed trepidation.

'Can you trust those men?' she asked. 'How do you know it isn't a false address?'

'Oh, I know,' Dan replied mysteriously. 'Like I said, I've got contacts. And anyway, even if it was a false address, I could always track those two down at the animal market. I don't think they've got any intention of doing a runner.'

'Of course.' Emma sank shakily back down on to the chair she had just vacated, shaking her head disbelievingly.

'They've got contacts at the airport, too,' she muttered. 'I had no idea the corruption ran so deep.'

As Dan also sat down, he looked at her.

'At least society over here is determined to tackle the problem. With little battles like this, they'll win the war,' he said, taking another swig of lager. 'Which reminds me, I've got some phone calls to make. Police and such,' he added under his breath.

Emma's eyes widened.

'I didn't realise you were working in co-operation with the police.'

'Actually, I've been in contact with them for weeks,' Dan admitted.

'Something else you omitted to tell me,' Emma said, with a trace of chagrin.

Dan sighed heavily, the conflict between them momentarily revived.

'Sorry, but I can't go blabbing left, right and centre. And not a word to Frost,' he added, raising a warning finger. 'I don't care what story you tell him about tomorrow, just make sure you shake him off. OK?'

'OK, as you wish, though he'll have to know eventually,' Emma replied coolly. 'I must admit, though,' she went on, relenting slightly, 'that I'm glad to learn your investigation is all official and above board.'

Dan was looking at her again. This time as she met his gaze the expression in his eyes was warm.

'Good,' he said and the atmosphere between them eased. 'Now, we'd better make a move. It's getting late and, like I said, I've got some calls to make, preferably in the privacy of my hotel room. On my mobile, of course. Actually,' Dan said, pausing suddenly, 'while we're about it, we might as well exchange mobile numbers, in case anything crops up.'

They dictated their numbers to each other, keying them in to their respective mobile phones. They emerged from the din of the bar into the muggy night.

'I'll hail us a taxi,' Dan said.

Emma laid a restraining hand on his arm.

'Just a minute, Dan.'

She glanced at the street around her, which was full of passing strangers, intent on their own business.

'Now we're alone together, or sort of, how about you put me fully in the picture about this deal? How about running me through the whole operation?'

'You're right,' he conceded finally. 'Maybe I have been unnecessarily cagey. It's an occupational hazard, I guess. I'm so used to being secretive, I'm finding it difficult to open up now that I've finally got a partner in crime.'

'I don't know why, but I kind of like being described as your partner in crime,' Emma said.

Dan smiled. They began to walk slowly down the street, pausing to look in the occasional lit shop window. Dan spoke in a low voice as they walked.

'The Thai police will be lying in wait at the airport tomorrow to arrest the dealers if they accompany us there. I've just got to ring them and confirm the details, the time and boarding gate. Police will also be waiting outside the dealers' yard, and will arrest them if necessary. If not, they'll search the dealers' yard while they're away, and maybe find more damning evidence.'

Dan looked at her meaningfully. 'That's the preferable of the two options, really. That's why it suits us if the dealers accompany us to the airport.'

'I see. Sorry, me and my big mouth, I nearly blabbed on that one. I assumed you wouldn't want them to accompany us.'

Emma thought of the two men, Lek and Gharma, and their wary brown eyes as they had done the deal, and felt a momentary twinge of guilt at deceiving them in this way. For many, life was hard, and they were only trying to earn a living. Then she thought of the baby orang-utans, and the guilt dispersed rapidly.

'You seem to have the whole thing planned meticulously, like a military operation,' she commented.

'That's right. Just call me General Fitzgerald,' he half-joked, sketching a mock-salute.

'What does that make me? Private Lombard?' Emma's smile was fleeting. She gave a brief shiver, though the air was as humid as ever.

'I just hope everything runs to plan tomorrow, and that nothing goes wrong.'

'It's all a matter of perfect timing, and

communication. Anyway, it's a standard procedure. The police capture many dealers in this way. The trouble is, though, that all too often, nothing comes of it in court.'

'That's a real shame,' Emma said. 'After so much hard work on everyone's part . . . you, the police, your contacts at the animal welfare group.'

'Hmm, yes, everyone's put in a lot of preparation work.'

Dan patted his black courier bag containing the camcorder, slung as ever over his shoulder.

'And this should help as evidence, too.'

A sudden thought occurred to Emma.

'You're not still filming now, are you?' she asked, dismayed as the prospect that her every word, their every bicker was being recorded.

Dan laughed gently.

'Of course not.'

Suddenly, in the doorway of a closed shop, he pulled her towards him. 'Now I wouldn't want to get this on film, would I?'

Tenderly, he kissed her. Feeling the passion flare between them, Emma was helpless to resist, and found herself returning the kiss. Eventually, it was Emma who pulled away.

'What is it?' Dan asked. 'It's Frost, isn't it?'

'No,' Emma replied instinctively. 'It's not that . . . well, I don't know . . .'

'You're right, Em,' Dan agreed. 'It's no good. We can't do this until you sort out the

90

situation between you and Frost.'

'There's nothing to sort out,' Emma said helplessly. 'As far as I'm concerned, it's over between Mark and me, and has been for ages.'

'So what made you suddenly get cold feet just then?'

'I don't know,' Emma repeated, groping for the words. 'But it's not about Mark. Like I said, that's over, finished.'

Dan looked cynical.

'That's not how he sees it. I can tell from the things he says, from the way he looks at you, at me.'

'Maybe you're right,' Emma said.

Secretly, though, she wondered if it suited her subconscious to use Mark as an excuse for other, deeper concerns she might have, concerns that might have been prompted at the thought that she and Dan were getting serious, fears prompted by what had happened to her parents; fears that no relationship, however promising, could ever last.

They both gazed at each other, with frustrated passion, and disappointment. It was several minutes before either of them recovered their composure sufficiently to hail a taxi, the taxi that would transport them back to the hotel, and reality.

CHAPTER SIX

A persistent ringing woke Emma from her dreams the following morning. It was not the landline phone, which had sat silently on her bedside table since she had arrived here, but her mobile which lay beside it. As she went to pick it up, Emma noticed that the time on her travel clock said twenty past seven. Ten minutes before her alarm was due to go off!

Her heart began to pound in anticipation as she clasped the slim phone. Would it be Dan or Mark?

' 'Morning, Emma.'

It was Dan. In spite of herself, Emma felt relieved. She felt, too, as if sleep had cleared the air between them. For now, she would think of Dan simply as a friend.

'Sorry to wake you,' he added.

'How did you guess?' Emma mumbled sleepily.

Dan chuckled. 'Anyway, apologies for the earliness of the hour. Are you up for it today then?'

'You bet,' Emma replied, with more conviction than she felt. Inwardly, she steeled herself to be brave.

'Good. I made a few calls last night,' Dan said. 'I would have called you, too, but I didn't want to disturb your beauty sleep.'

'I know, I know,' Emma wise-cracked. 'I need every minute I can get.'

Dan ignored this.

'So, I phoned the police. They'll have Orchid Road under surveillance, and they'll be ready to swing into action the minute they see us leaving the yard.' He paused for breath. 'I also rang the dealers to tell them we've booked our flights, and arranged for us to go round to the yard this morning and collect the animals.'

'So, what time are we supposedly flying out?'

'Our flight is supposedly due for take-off at twelve thirty this lunchtime. I took the precaution of ringing the airport to check what time there actually was a flight today. It's with Thai Airways, and the booking gate is number seven.'

Emma swallowed.

'What if the dealers check to see we're actually booked on to that flight?' she asked uneasily.

'They won't check,' Dan replied in his typical blunt way. 'And besides, we could have given them false names. Oh, yes, and, by the way, you'd better carry an overnight bag, just so it's plausible that we're travelling out of the country.'

Emma drew a long breath, marshalling her next question.

'So what's the exact plan of action for

today?'

Dan cleared his throat.

'Well, ideally, I'd like us to make quite an early start, but it all depends on how you're going to shake off old matey.'

'Hey, don't call Mark that!' Emma reproved lightly, but only half-heartedly. 'He's a creature of habit. Mark, I mean. If I know him, he'll be going down for breakfast at the same time as yesterday, eight-thirty on the dot, assuming he'll meet up with me down there, as happened yesterday morning, so that together we can make our plans for the day.'

'So if we aim to have finished breakfast by eight, quarter past at the latest,' Dan continued for her, 'we should be able to escape from the hotel before Frost surfaces.'

'Thus avoiding the need for any elaborate deceptions,' Emma finished. 'I must admit, I'm not too keen on lying to people,' she added.

'I know, Em. You've got a heart of gold.'

Emma frowned, unsure if Dan was teasing her.

'In any case, we'd better get cracking. I'll see you down in the dining-room in fifteen minutes?'

'See you there,' Emma confirmed, before hanging up.

It was strange having breakfast with Dan, Emma thought, glancing at him across the table. Somehow it was even more intimate than having dinner together.

Hastily she switched her thoughts. For now, she was going to push their personal relationship from her mind. Sure, there were problems between them, but for now she must concentrate on the business in hand. Dan was lifting his cup, draining the last of his coffee.

'I hate to rush you, Emma, but you'd better eat up.'

He glanced at his watch for the umpteenth time.

'It's nearly ten past eight now, and Frost could be down at any minute.'

'You're as bad as Mark himself,' she complained. 'He was always an absolute stickler for punctuality. The irony is that when I'm left to my own devices, I'm perfectly capable of being on time. I wouldn't be competent to run my own business otherwise.'

'Exactly,' Dan agreed.

'Mark and I are both organised kinds of people, you see,' Emma went on. 'That was one of the things we had in common.'

'Finished?' he asked abruptly. 'Sorry, Em,' he added gently. 'I don't want to give you indigestion, but things would be a whole lot easier if we didn't bump into your ex. I suppose I'm just a bit jumpy this morning. A lot is riding on this.'

'Well, I'm finished now,' Emma said.

She and Dan stood in unison, scraping back the chairs. Emma picked up her overnight bag. Dan slung his courier bag over his shoulder.

'Let's go.'

Emma glanced at her own watch as they were leaving the dining-room. 'Heavens!' she murmured. 'It's gone ten past.'

'Yes, well, I did try and tell you,' Dan muttered in his matter-of-fact way.

'Sorry,' Emma conceded, flicking him a glance. 'Yes, OK, maybe you did have a point. I guess I was so busy bickering with you that I was unaware of the time slipping by.'

'Apology accepted. Now, come on.'

Emma glanced at the elevators as they passed on their way to the hotel's marble-lined main entrance. The lift doors were closed, and there were a couple of guests waiting to go up to their room. Her heart began to pound.

'It's OK, no sign of your friend,' Dan muttered as they made stealthily towards the hotel's revolving doors.

'No,' Emma agreed. 'Oh, heck,' she said suddenly.

The lift doors had slid open, revealing Mark, morning-fresh, clad in his holiday uniform of beige shorts and white shirt, looking about him.

Emma hissed. 'There he is,' and at that moment, Mark seemed to glance in their direction.

'Has he seen us?' Dan muttered back.

'I don't know.'

Emma had no desire to find out, either. Without thinking, she grabbed Dan's hand, dragging him with her out through the doorway. Once outside, Emma leaned back against the wall of the hotel, giggling, with the half-hysterical relief of having made a narrow escape. Emma was still holding Dan's hand, inadvertently pulling him to her. For a moment he looked as if he wanted to kiss her, but the moment passed and he did not do so.

'No distractions, Emma,' he said, looking regretful. 'This is serious business.'

'I know that,' she replied.

'Sorry, Emma.'

'You don't have to apologise. It's fine by me.'

But it wasn't fine. Somehow this was the final straw in their awkward relationship. Emma felt rejected, and was reminded, too, of the unresolved problems between her and Dan.

'You wouldn't believe how nervous I am about today,' she said tightly. 'But I'm trying not to think about it.'

'That's a good strategy, Emma,' Dan said soothingly. 'Try to concentrate on the seriousness of the job in hand.'

'Of course I will, but I'd prefer it if you didn't patronise me.'

Indignant, Emma tried to tug her hand free but Dan held fast. Still holding her, Dan used his free hand to hail a taxi. Luckily, one pulled up instantly, and seconds later they were safely installed in the back.

Dan gave the driver the address and just as the taxi pulled away, Emma saw Mark emerging from the entrance of the hotel, and gaze from side to side down the street, looking bemused.

'Mark!' she hissed and Dan followed her gaze.

'Ah. So it is.'

At that moment, Emma's eye caught Mark's, and this time their gaze held.

Then the taxi sped her and Dan away.

'Poor Mark's going to be so mad at missing out on this expedition,' Emma murmured. 'He's missing out on the source material for potentially the most exciting part of his article!'

'Frost and his article can go to blazes,' Dan growled. 'We've got important work to do here. I've spent months building up to this and I don't want anything to ruin it.'

Emma gave Dan a pointed look but did not trust herself to say anything else. They subsided into a cool silence.

It was almost ten minutes later when the taxi dropped them off in Orchid Road.

As they got out, Dan muttered, 'It'll be interesting to see if we bump into anyone else around this yard. I have a feeling that our friends, Lek and Gharma, may not be the masterminds behind this operation.'

Number 21 was on the street corner, with a high fence running round the sides of the ramshackle property. Emma glanced down the road, assessing the parked vehicles she could see.

'I can't see any sign of the police,' she whispered, momentarily forgetting that she was mad at Dan.

'They'll be working undercover.'

'Oh, of course.'

'They won't want to look at all suspicious,' Dan added, looking around him. 'But they'll be there. At least, I hope they are.'

Lifting a hand, Dan banged on a tall wooden gate. After a minute or so, there was the sound of heavy bolts being scraped back. The gate was pulled open, and they came face to face with the short, stocky figure of Lek.

'Ah, hello,' he muttered.

'Hello.' Dan smiled. 'We've come to do business.'

Lek nodded. He glanced from side to side down the road, before letting them in. The gate slammed shut behind them. Lek drew large bolts across it, and Emma had the feeling that they were now trapped inside, that there was no going back. Dan cleared his throat.

'Can we see the orang-utans?' he asked politely.

He was obviously trying to sound relaxed,

but Emma could sense the tension in the air.

Lek nodded minutely. 'Follow me.'

There was the sound of hammering as Lek led them across the large yard. Emma observed that he seemed exceptionally nervous, wary and she was glad to walk in Dan's large, comforting shadow.

They passed various animals and birds in cages, from brightly-coloured parrots to tortoises and small monkeys. The sun blazed down on them. As they walked, the sound of hammering grew louder, drowning out the chattering of birds and beasts.

'There they are,' Lek announced, flourishing one hand, and then standing back.

There, in two small cages, were little bald babies, their cute faces surrounded by orange fuzz. Emma's heart went out to them.

'Hello, again,' she murmured, rushing forward to the cages and kneeling down in front of them, 'My, you've both grown since I last saw you.'

'They certainly have.'

Dan had also stepped forward, appraising the animals with a critical eye. 'But don't let that fool you. They're still very young, of course.'

'They are now four months old,' Lek said, hanging back a little. 'One male, one female, as I believe we confirmed on the phone, Mr Ferguson.'

Emma wasn't surprised to hear that Dan's

alias extended to his surname. Emma and Dan continued to gaze concernedly at the animals for several silent minutes.

'They seem to be in good condition,' Dan said guardedly, still staring at them.

Emma nodded.

'Yes, they seem OK, in my unprofessional opinion, though what would I know?'

'Don't be like that, Elizabeth,' Dan said in a low voice.

Emma stood up, brushing the dust off her cream cotton shorts and her long, slim brown legs. Her eyes were reluctant to leave the young animals, whose round, brown eyes gazed out through the bars of their cages. Suddenly, though, she caught sight of the source of the hammering. Gharma was over in the corner of the yard, bent over what looked like a small, rough, wooden box, banging nails into it. There was a pile of scrap wood beside him, from which he was constructing the boxes.

Unable to stop herself, Emma nudged Dan's arm.

'Is Gharma making what I think he's making?' she murmured.

Dan followed the direction of her gaze.

'Yes,' he replied tonelessly.

'Surely they're not going to put the animals in those tiny, rough boxes?' Emma persisted, dismayed.

Lek intercepted her look.

'Don't worry yourself, Elizabeth,' he reassured her. 'Your orang-utans will be fine.'

But he didn't exactly look relaxed himself, Emma observed, not for the first time that day. He looked so edgy, did he suspect that the whole deal was a set-up, that maybe even now the police were lurking outside the yard?

Gharma came over, carrying the two boxes, one on top of the other. He said something in Thai to Lek, then added, 'Good morning, Dave, Elizabeth.'

He looked as serious and wary as Lek, his charm of the previous evening all but vanished.

'Good morning, Gharma,' Emma replied, smiling, trying her best to be pleasant and casual.

Lek, who had momentarily disappeared, returned carrying a plastic drinks bottle with a nozzle-type lid.

'A little home-made sedative,' he explained, brandishing the bottle at Emma and Dan. 'If we give the animals a heavy dose now, they will stay quiet on the journey, both to the airport, and once you get on the aeroplane.'

'Really?' Emma shuddered.

'Hang on a minute. May I?' Dan asked, taking the bottle from Lek who, caught unawares, did not resist.

Dan unscrewed the cap of the bottle, sniffing the contents. He reeled back, replacing the lid.

'I can assure you it is effective,' Lek was saying. 'One dose should be enough, but you may need to give the animals another, should they start to become lively.'

'No,' Dan said suddenly, his voice sharp.

Both men turned to stare at him in surprise. Emma did, too. Knowing Dan as well as she now felt she did, Emma saw him make a clear effort to reel in his temper, to retain a pleasant exterior.

'I mean,' Dan continued, his dark eyes creased into a constrained smile, 'I'm a little concerned. I'm worried that if we give such young animals a heavy dose now, it will do them great harm.'

Emma, feeling anxious and aware of the desperate situation for the animals, took up Dan's thread.

'I can't help agreeing with Dave,' she beamed, trying to work some feminine charm. 'Perhaps if we wait until we are at the airport, then the animals will not need such a heavy dose.'

Lek and Gharma exchanged glances.

'Very well,' Gharma said slowly. 'But if you do so, it will be necessary for us to accompany you to the airport.'

There was a momentary pause.

'OK,' Dan said eventually.

'It will cost you extra,' Lek added quickly. 'Another two hundred pounds.'

'Very well,' Dan replied guardedly and

reached into his pocket, pulled out a wad of notes and peeled off four fifties.

'We will travel in our car.'

Lek took the money from Dan, stuffing it into his pocket. He turned to Gharma.

'Are the boxes ready?'

Gharma nodded, proffering the wooden boxes. Lek produced a ring of keys from his pocket, then bent to unlock the first of the two cages.

'That's the female,' Dan told Emma, as Lek took the smaller of the two animals out of its cage.

A sudden thought struck her.

'Haven't they got names?' she asked no-one in particular and was met with disinterested shrugs and shakes of the head.

'You may call them whatever you wish,' Gharma said, with an echo of yesterday evening's charming smile. 'They belong to you and your friend now.'

Emma looked helplessly at Dan, who shrugged and said, 'Any ideas, Lizzie?'

Emma hesitated, wondering if it was a good idea to get too attached to these animals. It was as if Dan read her thoughts.

'They deserve the dignity of a name,' he told her quietly.

'How about Jade for the girl?' she suggested presently.

'Fine,' Dan said. 'And the male?'

Emma gazed at the male, at a loss. She

looked at his vivid, orange-red hair.

'How about Rufus?' she said finally and Dan smiled faintly, nodding.

Emma watched, her heart in her mouth, as Lek lowered the female into the wooden box. Like her brother, little Jade was trusting, too trusting, as she allowed herself to be placed in the empty box, with only a token squeal as protest.

'Hang on a minute,' Emma exclaimed, rushing to pluck a handful of greenery from a tree that overhung the yard.

She placed that, plus the small dish of chopped fruit from the cage, into the bottom of the wooden box.

'There. Somehow it makes the thing look marginally less spartan.'

Gharma proceeded to nail a wooden lid on to the box. Emma was thankful that at least Jade had a small, chicken-wire window to peep out of. Now it was the turn of the little male, Rufus. As Lek removed him from his cage, Rufus's eyes looked very round and startled, and he seemed fidgety, more bothered than his sister had been. Dan moved forward to stroke the top of the animal's head.

'There's a boy,' he murmured reassuringly. 'It'll be OK.'

Emma gazed at Dan in surprise. It was the closest she had seen to him treating an animal with sentimentality. Unable to stop herself, Emma, too, moved forward, instinctively wanting to touch the animal.

'He's gorgeous, isn't he?' she said softly to Dan.

Lek intercepted Emma's look, and it was as if something in him relented.

'Would you like to hold him?'

'Go ahead,' Dan told her. 'It might calm the little chap down, being held for a few moments.'

Carefully, Emma took the baby orang-utan from Lek, cradling the little animal in her arms. He was so much like a little bald baby, with a smattering of orange fuzz. The tiny body stilled in her arms, and seemed to relax. It made Emma's heart dissolve, and she wondered if some dormant maternal instinct was being awakened.

'Oh, he's so sweet,' she breathed.

'I know, I know,' Dan muttered from beside her. 'It's just like when you held your sister's babies.'

Emma looked up at him in surprise.

'Fancy you remembering,' she said, with a half-smile.

Lek coughed abruptly, glancing at his watch.

'It is nearly ten o'clock now. Your flight is at, what, half twelve? You need time to check in. We must take care that you do not miss it,' he said, sounding restless and impatient once again.

Reluctantly, Emma handed little Rufus

back to Lek, who placed him into the second wooden box.

'Don't forget this.'

Emma quickly put in some greenery, and Dan supplied the animal's food dish, before Gharma moved forward to hammer down the wooden lid.

'And now we place the boxes inside the bags,' Gharma said, producing two faded barrel bags.

Emma glanced anxiously at Dan.

'But surely they'll suffocate?'

The day was stiflingly warm. Dan ran a hand through his cropped hair, a gesture that echoed her own anxiety.

But he just said, 'The bags will be left open, of course. Won't they?'

His tone addressed to the dealers, was more of a command than a question. Lek glanced quickly at him.

'OK. Until we reach the airport. Then the bags must be kept zipped up, until you and the animals are safely on to the aeroplane. Understood?'

'Of course.' Dan nodded briefly.

Gharma glanced at his watch.

'And now we had better get going. Dave, Elizabeth, you take a bag each. The car is parked outside.'

Shouldering her overnight bag, Emma picked up the barrel bag containing little Rufus, while Dan took the one containing

Jade.

'This way,' Gharma rallied them, brandishing his car keys, while Lek undid the bolts on the gate.

Carefully cradling her bag, Emma followed the dealers out to the rusty white estate which was parked in the street. Dan walked beside her, and they exchanged glances. Gharma unlocked the driver's door, slipping into the driver's seat and reaching across to unlock the other doors.

'You two, in the back,' Lek ordered them twitchily, and again he glanced up and down the street, as if fearing they were being watched.

'Good grief,' Dan growled as he and Emma scrambled in to the back of the car. 'It's hot in here.'

'You're telling me,' Emma muttered back, blowing her fringe away from her face, and as Lek got into the passenger seat she turned to Dan. 'Do you think the animals will be all right?'

'We'll just have to pray they will be,' Dan said darkly.

Lek glanced round at them over his shoulder, shooting them a quelling glance.

'Everything OK?' he asked as Gharma revved up the engine.

'Yes, fine,' Dan and Emma said in unison.

There was a muffled squeak from inside Emma's bag. She cradled it more carefully than ever.

'If not,' Lek continued, waggling the plastic drinks bottle, 'I have the sedative here.'

'No, everything's fine for now,' Dan repeated firmly.

The car swerved off round the corner of Orchid Road.

'All right, darling,' Emma murmured into her bag.

There was a small, reassuring flurry of movement within. Looking up to gaze out of the window, Emma looked in vain for the police cars that were supposed to be waiting in the street. Dan seemed tense and silent. The car paused at a junction, then turned left, out on to a busy road, following the sign to the airport. Emma, who was behind Gharma, peered over his shoulder at the gauges and dials on the dashboard. Horrified, Emma spoke to the occupants of the car in general

'It's ninety-two degrees in this car! Surely that's too hot for these little animals to be stuck in bags?'

Dan looked concerned, but only said, 'Hush, Elizabeth.' His tone implied the added words, 'Stay calm, or you could blow this for us.'

Sure enough Lek's head swung round again.

'It's OK, Elizabeth,' he said, sounding more edgy and impatient than ever. 'Do not worry about the animals. Dave,' he added warningly to Dan, 'Your friend asks a lot of questions, doesn't she?'

Chastened, Emma lapsed into silence. She glanced at her watch. It was now nearly eleven o'clock, and the heat seemed to be rising all the time. A bead of sweat trickled down her brow, and she wiped it away.

'Rather warm, isn't it?' Dan asked rhetorically.

The car went round another corner, and they all lurched to the side. Feeling the weight of the bag shift on her lap, Emma peeped inside. All seemed still and quiet within. Emma's heart skipped a beat, and she had the horrible feeling that something had happened to the little male orang-utan.

CHAPTER SEVEN

In the front, Lek and Gharma spoke to each other in Thai. Emma took advantage of the opportunity. 'Rufus is very quiet,' she said softly to Dan. 'How is Jade?'

'I can feel her moving about,' Dan replied.

'I can't feel Rufus. Dan, I'm worried about him.'

Peeling back the edges of the bag, Emma peered into the wooden box. Still all was quiet. Suddenly panicking, Emma rummaged for the comb in her overnight bag. Finding it, she slid it underneath the rough wooden box-lid. Fortunately it had been hastily fixed in place with only two nails and she felt the wood give. Using the comb as a lever, she managed to prise the lid open. Dan saw what she was doing.

'Careful, Lizzie,' he warned, his voice a hiss.

But Emma had the lid off now and to her intense relief, Rufus's head popped up out of the box.

'Oh, darling, you're OK,' she muttered, stroking the orang-utan's little head. 'Thank goodness.'

The next few seconds passed in a flash. Before she knew what was happening, Rufus had escaped from his box and was off, crawling around the car. Emma's heart plummeted.

'Oh, no!' she murmured in dismay, leaning forward to grab the animal who slipped through her grasp.

'Elizabeth,' Dan said, the colour draining from his rugged, tanned face. 'I told you to be careful!'

Lek turned round and saw what had happened. He, too, tried to grab Rufus. 'One of the animals has escaped from the box! This is not good news.'

In response, Gharma swerved the car violently, almost crashing it. He steadied it with another swerve and continued driving.

Emma made another desperate lunge for Rufus but again he escaped her, darting through to the front of the car. Lek grabbed him and this time was successful. Saying something in Thai, Lek reached for the bottle of home-made sedative.

'No!' Dan and Emma exclaimed in unison, leaning forward.

Before Dan or Emma could stop him, Lek had squirted some of the sedative into Rufus's mouth. After just a few seconds, Rufus seemed to wilt, growing sleepy.

'Maybe he'll go back in his box now,' Emma suggested, her heart pounding with anxiety. 'Can I take him, please?'

Leaning forward, she took the animal from Lek, who relinquished him reluctantly with a wary look. Once she had Rufus back in her arms, Emma did not put him in the box but held him tight, vowing she wouldn't ever let him go again.

There was a scuffle from inside Dan's bag.

'What about the other animal?' Lek asked instantly, his head swinging round. 'Oh, she's sleeping,' Dan lied quickly. 'She's fine.'

Still looking uneasy, Lek turned back to the front of the car and said something in Thai to Gharma. Gharma made some reply, clenching the steering-wheel, his eyes on the road in front of him. Lek turned back to Dan and Emma.

'It's no good! The trouble with the animals is a bad sign, a bad omen.'

Dan leaned forward, speaking quickly but calmly.

'Come, come, Lek. It will be all right, I'm sure. The animals are under control now.'

In spite of herself, Emma had to admire his coolness under pressure. Lek shook his dark, curly head.

'No. It is no good today. Tomorrow, maybe.'

'But, Lek,' Dan implored him, as Emma observed the exchange in dismay. 'We've booked our flights back to the UK! Everything is arranged.'

Suddenly Gharma swerved the car into a left-hand turning, doing a rapid three-point turn before pulling back out on to the main road, back in the direction they had come.

'You will have to cancel the flights,' Lek said. 'Re-book them for tomorrow.'

In the back of the sweltering car, Emma and Dan exchanged resigned looks. Emma widened her eyes at him, in a silent question as to what on earth they were going to do now.

'I must phone my partner at the zoo, back in the UK,' Dan said loudly to the car in general. 'Inform him that everything is off for today and will be postponed, possibly until tomorrow.'

Emma glanced at Dan's inscrutable face as he reached for his mobile phone and keyed in a number. She strongly suspected that this partner was imaginary and that instead, Dan was phoning the police to warn them that they were heading back to the yard.

'Hello?' Dan said into the phone. 'Yes, we're in the car with the animals right now but unfortunately there have been a few complications. Where are you right now? I see. Yes, hopefully we will go for it tomorrow. Goodbye.'

Dan severed the connection, ending the call. Emma mopped the perspiration from her brow. The car seemed to be growing more stuffy than ever as, outside, the noonday sun rose in the sky. She looked down at Rufus on her lap and a cold hand clenched her heart. The little animal's eyes were almost closed. She felt sick with guilt that, thanks to her stupidity, Lek had administered the sedative

114

to Rufus.

'He looks very sleepy,' she said.

'Jade, too,' Dan reported, removing Jade's box from the bag so that she could get more of the meagre air supply. 'Pass me that comb, please,' he ordered Emma.

She did so and Dan levered the lid off Jade's box, taking her out to hold her in his arms.

'Is she OK?' Emma asked.

Dan shrugged.

'Both animals are looking very drowsy. I'm concerned that in this hot, airless environment, they could soon lose consciousness.'

'Oh, Dan,' Emma muttered in dismay. 'I'm so sorry about putting Rufus in danger. Please, you've got to do something to save him, and Jade.'

'Don't worry,' Dan said tersely, 'I intend to.'

He leaned forward to the front of the car, clearing his throat.

'Lek, is there any chance that we could stop somewhere and give these animals some air?'

Lek looked regretful.

'Sorry, but no. The omens are bad and we cannot take any further chances today.'

'But we'd got nearly all the way to the airport!' Dan protested, sounding as close to angry as Emma had heard him. 'Now we'll have to go all the way back to the yard and I'm not sure the animals can last the distance in his stuffy car.'

He gestured towards the dashboard with a stabbing finger. 'Look at the temperature in here.'

'I'm sorry,' Lek replied resignedly. 'There is nothing I can do about it.' Despairing, Emma turned imploring eyes on Dan.

'Don't worry,' he whispered to her. 'I'm monitoring the situation. As a qualified vet, I'll do everything in my power not to let these animals die.'

Emma wished she could believe him.

The journey back to the yard seemed stiflingly hot and endless. Emma kept her eyes on the sleepy little orang-utan in her arms, only lifting her gaze from time to time to exchange an anxious glance with Dan. She wondered if he was thinking the same thing as her. Part of her longed to make the dealers stop the car, to release them and the animals, for her and Dan to confess everything if necessary, anything to ensure that the baby orang-utans didn't die in this stuffy, overheated car.

But the other half of her knew that, if they did this, the dealers might not let them keep the orang-utans. And heaven knew what would happen to the animals then. So maybe it was best to try and see this whole thing through.

116

Back in his hotel room after breakfast, Mark Frost paced the floor restlessly. For the umpteenth time he wondered what the heck Emma was up to, gadding about with Fitzgerald first thing in the morning, holding hands, no less. Oh, yes, he'd seen her. They'd been clever, those two, sneaking off without him, but not clever enough.

Impatiently, Mark loosened the top button of his shirt. He felt too hot, as he always did in this country and uncomfortable. Thinking about Emma was unsettling him. He hoped that she wouldn't get herself mixed up in any kind of trouble involving this illegal animal export business

For his own part, Mark still didn't entirely trust Fitzgerald. But he sensed that Emma was growing more and more attached to the man and there was nothing he could do about it.

There was a knock at the door. Mark went and pulled it open.

It was the chambermaid, with an apologetic smile.

'Oh, sorry, shall I come back later?'

Mark shook his head.

'No, it's fine. I'm just about to leave.'

He had to get out—go somewhere, anywhere.

117

*　　*　　*

At last the car swung back into the familiar territory of Orchid Road. Emma noticed that there was no sign of any police cars in the street. She looked at Dan who was glancing out of the windows in consternation, apparently thinking exactly the same as her.

'We're here, anyway,' Dan said. 'Thank goodness for that.'

As soon as Gharma had pulled on the handbrake, Emma and Dan scrambled out of the car. Today, the humid air seemed blissfully fresh, sweet as nectar, in comparison to the baking interior of the vehicle. Lek and Gharma rushed ahead of them to unlock the gate to the yard, Emma and Dan following behind with the sleepy orang-utans in their arms.

'Where are the police?' Emma whispered urgently to Dan.

'They said they'd get here as soon as possible,' Dan whispered back. 'They said on the phone that there had been another emergency so they were running late.'

'Oh, no.'

'Just do me a favour, Emma,' Dan whispered. 'Once we get inside the yard, keep the dealers talking for me. Show them photos of your nephew and niece, do a song and dance routine,' he went on desperately, 'anything to distract them.'

There was no time to ask Dan what he was planning to do.

'Just be careful, Dan,' Emma begged, her heart quickening with anxiety.

Gharma held the gate open for them, turning round to see where they'd got to. As his gaze flickered suspiciously over them, Emma and Dan lapsed into silence.

'Inside, quick,' Gharma said, his eyes darting up and down the street.

He slammed the gate shut behind them. They were back in the yard amongst the cages of squawking, brightly-coloured parrots and chattering monkeys.

'I'm very concerned about Rufus, Gharma,' Emma said, as Lek disappeared into the house.

She still felt sick with guilt over her irresponsible actions.

'Oh, don't worry about him,' Gharma said, with what he clearly hoped was a reassuring smile. 'I'm sure the fresh air will revive him presently. How about the female? How is she doing?'

'I'm not sure,' Dan said, playing the innocent. 'You probably know more about these animals than I do.'

'Here, let me hold her,' Gharma said. 'Let me have a look.'

Dan handed little Jade over to Gharma, then melted quietly away into the background.

'What do you think?' Emma asked Gharma

confidingly. 'Does Jade look OK to you?'

If it wasn't such a desperate situation, it would be bizarre. There they stood, like two new mothers comparing babies.

'A little sleepy perhaps.' Gharma's casual manner could not disguise his concern. 'But I think she, too, will be all right now she is out of the car.'

'Let's hope so.'

Out of the corner of her eye, Emma was aware of Dan, standing at the far end of the yard, speaking urgently into his mobile phone. Marvelling at Dan's bravery, she prayed Gharma would not turn round and see him.

She was relieved when, moments later, Dan materialised back behind Gharma's shoulder.

'Ah, Dave, there you are,' Gharma said, eyeing him suspiciously.

Emma hoped fervently he wouldn't suspect what Dan had been up to. For his part, Dan didn't look too happy.

'Here, let me look at Rufus,' he barked, his brow creased in consternation.

Wordlessly, Emma handed him the sleepy orang-utan. Dan pressed his forefinger to the animal's wrist. When he looked up, his eyes were dark with concern.

'Rufus's pulse rate has slowed dramatically. This animal's life could be in serious danger.'

Emma glanced at Jade, still being held by Gharma.

'Jade doesn't look too good either but at

least there's a bit more life in her.'

'It was that blasted home-made sedative!' Dan said, his voice shaking with barely-suppressed fury. 'I should never have allowed Lek to give it to the creature.'

'No, Dave, don't blame yourself,' Emma burst out. 'It was my fault, for letting Rufus escape from his box,'

'And the temperature in that car was far too hot for these young animals,' Dan went on, ignoring her plea of culpability. 'Animals should never be transported in those conditions.'

Gharma's good-looking face looked distinctly uneasy. He handed the female orang-utan back to Emma.

'Here, Elizabeth, you had better take her for a moment. Speaking of my friend, Lek, I had better go and see where he has got to. You two will stay right where you are, of course.'

'Of course,' Dan said impatiently.

As soon as Gharma had disappeared toward the house, Emma turned urgently to Dan.

'I think Gharma might be getting suspicious. Did you manage to make your phone calls?'

Dan nodded.

'The police and a local vet. These animals need to be rehydrated fast. Hopefully that vet should be here any second now.'

121

He glanced down at Rufus who looked limp and lifeless, his eyes closed. 'If not, it could be too late for this little chap.'

Emma's eyes filled with tears but she fought back the urge to cry. Her earlier disagreement with Dan was now completely forgotten, overshadowed by far more important things.

'Oh, Dan,' she whispered, gazing across at the small male orang-utan. 'He's got to be OK. He's just got to.'

At that moment, there was the sound of tyres screeching in the road outside, followed by car doors slamming. Emma heard running footsteps then the sound of someone hammering on the yard gate. The voice said something in Thai, then a voice said in English, 'Police. Open up.'

There was no sign of Lek or Gharma. The hammering intensified.

'Shouldn't we open the gate?'

Emma glanced questioningly at Dan. Dan shook his head.

'Play dumb,' he muttered under his breath. 'Pretend you're surprised to see them.'

Finally there was the sound of splintering wood as the gate was forced open, busting open the metal bolts. Four uniformed policemen burst in, followed by a small, dark-haired man carrying a large black case. The vet! He rushed straight over to Dan and Emma. Dan spoke rapidly yet clearly to him, using frantic hand gestures to back up his words.

'Two orang-utans, four months old, one male, one female, both overheated and dehydrated. This one, the male, appears to be in the most danger. He was given some kind of home-made sedative. I'm not sure of the ingredients. He's very drowsy and his pulse rate is dangerously low.'

The vet gave both animals a brief inspection.

'We must waste no time,' he said urgently, glancing at Dan. 'You will help me, yes?'

'Of course,' Dan nodded. 'I have some experience in this line of work.'

The vet, working with the assistance of Dan and, to a lesser extent, Emma, proceeded to insert a drip into the arm of each orang-utan. Meanwhile, Emma could not help but be aware of what was going on around her. The place appeared to be disintegrating into chaos. More policemen were arriving, some seizing the cages containing animals and removing them from the yard. Other policemen disappeared into the ramshackle house.

'Now,' the vet said, looking down at the two sleeping orang-utans, 'I must take these animals away to my surgery. They are very sick, in need of consistent medical attention. But then, sir, if you have veterinary experience, you will know that. The male has maybe a fifty-fifty chance of survival, the female possibly a little better than that.'

Emma's heart lurched in dismay. Fifty-fifty!

She gazed down at Jade then across at Rufus.

'Come on, you two,' she willed them. 'You've got to make it.'

If not, it'll be partly my fault, she added mentally, and it will haunt me for the rest of my life.

'We'll come with you,' Dan told the vet. 'I'm anxious to monitor the animals' progress.'

At that moment, a slight scuffle distracted their attention. Two policemen came out of the back door of the house. Lek was handcuffed to one, Gharma to the other.

As they approached Emma and Dan, Lek's brown eyes were reproachful.

'You set this up,' he shouted. 'It was all a trap.'

'No wonder the omens were bad,' Gharma added bitterly.

'A trap?' Dan frowned, contriving a look of bemusement. 'No, no, you've got it wrong. Believe you me,' he said heavily, 'the last thing I wanted was for the police to turn up today.'

Emma recalled his instructions to play dumb. She widened her eyes in a show of anxiety.

'Oh, Dave,' she wailed, glancing at him. 'What are we going to do?'

'Shame on you, Dave,' Gharma muttered,

'for bringing your woman into this.'

Dan glanced at Gharma but ignored the remark. Instead, he said slowly, 'Try to stay calm, Elizabeth. I was hoping for us to accompany the animals to the vet's, but I fear now that this may not be possible.'

'Your friend is right, miss,' a policeman said, approaching Emma and taking the male orang-utan from her.

Another policeman moved forward, clapping some handcuffs on to her wrist.

'I'm afraid the two of you are under arrest for attempting to illegally export endangered animals out of the country. You do not have to say anything, but anything you do say may be used in evidence.'

Emma felt the cold metal of the handcuff close around her warm wrist. She'd never been arrested before. She just prayed that Dan was right and that this was all a set-up, a bit of play-acting to convince the dealers that she and Dan were innocent, to protect their lives. The only trouble was, this all felt horribly realistic.

There was the sound of more raised voices from the house, another scuffle, and then another policeman appeared, handcuffed to a slight, well-dressed man, whom Emma did not recognise.

'Chatichai,' Lek muttered under his breath, his voice flat and lifeless.

Emma glanced at Dan and the look of

125

barely-concealed triumph in his eyes told her all she needed to know. This was the shady mastermind figure whose existence Dan had suspected all along. This was the boss of the whole operation.

CHAPTER EIGHT

Emma sat next to Dan on the back seat of the car, gazing out of the window as they sped along. 'This is a beautiful, fascinating country,' she mused, 'and I'd like to return one day, in happier circumstances.'

'Me, too,' Dan agreed.

After a pause, Emma added, in some relief, 'Thank heavens this is a taxi, not a police car.'

Briefly, Dan placed a hand on hers.

'You didn't think we were being arrested for real, did you?' he asked, his voice soft with concern. 'I told you to play dumb.'

Emma's mouth twisted.

'Oh, you know me. That's not something I find difficult,' she said with a wry grin.

Dan ignored that comment as the taxi took a corner.

'It was essential that we acted the innocents, both for your own safety, and to cover our tracks.'

His voice was serious and his gaze distant. For a moment he seemed far away from her.

'Anyway,' Emma said, as the car nosed into the heavy traffic, nearing the centre of Bangkok, 'I must say I'm relieved not to end up languishing in a foreign jail.'

After the police had taken Lek, Gharma and their boss, Chatichai, away, they had confiscated all the animals from the yard, before releasing Emma and Dan. Emma's heart was still pounding from the experience, and her forehead was damp with perspiration.

'What's going to happen to all those animals from the yard?' Emma asked Dan now.

'Well, firstly they'll be taken to a place of quarantine, before probably being given to some kind of zoo or animal sanctuary.'

Emma leaned back against the seat of the taxi, feeling some of the tension start to drain out of her.

'And to think that is what you do for a living, Dan, when you're not concentrating on the day job, that is.'

She wanted to tell him that she thought he was incredibly brave, but, mindful of their earlier falling out, couldn't find the words to do so.

Dan looked into her eyes, his rugged face looking tired but elated.

'Doesn't it make you feel good, though, when you succeed in what you've set out to do?'

'It certainly does,' Emma agreed.

'We just have to hope now that convictions are obtained for all three of those men.'

'And even if they are,' Emma added, 'I suppose that what we've done today has only foiled one small centre of the illegal animal trade.'

'That's right. And it somewhat takes the edge off the sense of satisfaction, to know that there are still two baby orang-utans whose lives hang in the balance.' Dan's eyes darkened with guilt. 'And that my own actions may have contributed to the gravity of their condition.'

Now it was Emma's turn to lay a comforting hand on Dan's.

'Oh, come on, Dan. You can't think like that. And anyway,' she went on, feeling that familiar surge of guilt, 'what about me? I was the one who let Rufus escape from his box, so that Lek gave him the sedative.'

'But you're a novice in this field, Emma. I'm responsible for your actions, because I allowed you to come along on the operation.'

'Oh, nonsense, Dan!' Emma burst out. 'I'm far guiltier than you are. But there's no point torturing ourselves with that, now.'

Dan turned deep brown, anguished eyes on her.

'Yes, but what if the orang-utans die, Emma? What if they die because I didn't insist the dealers stop the car and let us out? Because I was more bothered about securing their convictions than the lives of innocent, individual animals?'

Impulsively Emma squeezed Dan's fingers.

'You mustn't think like that,' she repeated. 'I've only played a small part in this operation, though I'd like to do more in the future.

129

You've got a lifelong commitment to it.'

The taxi swerved round a corner, tilting them both to one side, causing Emma's knee to brush against Dan's. The contact reminded her of the electrical tension between them, but she pushed it from her mind.

'If it wasn't for people like you, Dan, there would be far more suffering and frightened animals than there are in the world today.'

Dan sighed heavily.

'Maybe. It's kind of you to say so, Emma.' He ran a hand over his face. 'But whatever, our work isn't done. There's plenty still to do elsewhere.'

'Exactly.'

Skilfully, Emma turned the conversation to a subject she'd been wanting to tackle for some minutes.

'That's where people like Mark come in, writing their articles for newspapers, publicising the plight of animals around the world, raising people's awareness.'

A thunderous look passed across Dan's face, and his mood suddenly seemed to worsen irretrievably.

'I might have known you'd bring Frost into it sooner or later, Emma,' he grunted. 'That man's never far from your thoughts, is he?'

'Oh, Dan, for goodness' sake.'

His remark brought back to the surface all the unresolved issues between the two of them. Emma took a deep breath, trying to retain her calmness.

'Now, you know that's not true, and if you weren't in such a fraught mood you wouldn't even say it. However,' she went on, looking Dan in the eye, 'I do feel bad about running away from Mark earlier, and I think we owe it to him to update him on the situation sooner or later, whether or not you are going to allow him to write his article yet.'

'Not yet, Emma,' Dan barked, his eyes hollow and heavily shadowed with tiredness. 'It's much too soon for the article. It could jeopardise everything. Frost will have to wait until the cases have been brought to court and the convictions have been secured.'

'OK,' Emma said slowly. 'But you will agree for us both to meet up with him over dinner and explain everything?'

'I suppose so,' Dan said curtly.

'Tonight? Eight o'clock?' she persisted.

There was a pause.

'It may not be the best idea. But all right then, if you insist.'

Suddenly, Emma's pent-up exasperation burst free.

'You could be a bit more gracious about it, Dan! I know you're tired and emotional, but we've both been through a lot today, not just you.'

'Maybe you shouldn't have come along if you couldn't hack it, Emma,' Dan suggested coolly, eyeing her.

He was needling her, and this was the final straw, making Emma seethe.

'I'm still mad at you from earlier, by the way, Daniel Fitzgerald. I haven't forgotten!'

'Can you remember what exactly you're mad about, though?' he said sarcastically.

'Of course,' Emma shot back.

How to explain, though, that sense of being consistently rejected that she got from Dan, together with her own insecurities, not to mention the mess of their misunderstandings about Mark?

'Of course I haven't forgotten why,' she repeated and she thought of little Jade and Rufus. 'It's just that, for a while, other, more important things got in the way.'

Suddenly the mood between them altered again.

'Hmm. That reminds me,' Dan said, anxious lines returning to etch his face. 'I must call the vet for an update on the orang-utan's condition.'

He reached for his mobile phone. Just then the marble façade of the Indira Hotel loomed up before them.

'Well? Are you going to phone him now?' Emma asked, desperate to hear how the animals were getting on.

Dan shook his head, gesturing out of the window of the taxi.

'We're here now.' He gathered his courier bag to him. 'I might as well do it from my hotel room.'

'Don't shut me out, Dan,' she wanted to say. 'I'm emotionally involved in this whole thing too, now.'

But, with the new coolness that had sprung up between them, she found it impossible to say so.

Mark was out when Emma got back into the hotel, so she left a message at Reception for him to meet her and Dan for dinner at eight that evening.

After resting in her room, Emma showered away the tensions of the day, and changed into her sarong-dress before making her way down to the crowded dining-room. Glancing at her watch, she saw that it was five to eight. To her surprise, she glimpsed Dan amongst the diners, already waiting for them at the table. His grey shirt and shower-damp, spiky hair made him look refreshed, smart and handsome, not nearly as stressed and haggard as earlier.

Suddenly he looked up.

'Good evening, Emma,' he smiled, seeing her.

From the lurch her heart gave at the sight of him, Emma realised that her feelings for Dan had irrevocably turned into love, a love that meant that nothing else mattered, not Mark, nor what had happened to her parents' marriage. Her sister, Jane, was happily married, after all, so it could be done, not that

Emma would ever get the chance to test the strength of her love for Dan, to see if it stood the test of time . . .

'Good evening, Dan.' Emma approached the table a little awkwardly. 'Seems we're both early tonight.'

'It does indeed, Emma.'

Standing up to pull out her chair, Dan viewed her with something—was it apprehension in his eyes? They both sat, tucking their chairs up to the table.

'Well, here we are, then,' Emma said, for something to say.

There was an air of polite restraint now between them, after their heated exchanges in the taxi.

'I would have called you earlier,' Dan went on, eyeing her across an expanse of linen and gleaming glassware, 'but I was afraid you might be resting.'

'Oh, yes,' Emma said with a wry smile. 'I know how anxious you are about me needing all my beauty sleep.'

Dan gave a half-smile in return.

'I just thought you might want to know the outcome of my phone call to the vet. I'm sorry I gave you such short shrift earlier.'

'Don't worry about it,' Emma said, agog now, her heart pounding. 'Go on, then. Don't keep me in suspense. What did the vet say?'

Dan took a deep breath. He looked serious, and Emma prepared herself to hear the worst.

Suddenly she felt certain that Rufus hadn't made it.

'It was touch and go for a while,' Dan said, 'especially as far as Rufus was concerned, but both he and Jade are holding their own now. Jade is off the drip, but the vet won't know until tomorrow, for sure, if Rufus is going to pull through.'

Emma didn't realise she had been holding her breath until now, when she let some of it out in cautious relief.

'Well, that's good news, of sorts,' she said hesitantly, 'that he's holding. For a moment there, I was afraid you were going to say that Rufus had died.'

'No. He's hanging on in there. He must be a fighter.'

Dan clasped Emma's hand that was resting on the tablecloth. Tears filled her eyes, and if she wasn't mistaken, they glinted in Dan's, too.

'We might even be allowed to visit them tomorrow,' Dan added gruffly. 'If neither Rufus nor Jade have a relapse, that is.'

'Oh, I hope we can visit them,' Emma replied longingly. 'I can't bear the thought that I might never see the two of them again.'

There was a brief, awkward lull in the conversation. Emma wondered what to say after such an emotional scene, how she could use this thaw to start building bridges between them. Then she and Dan both spoke at once.

'Dan, I'm sorry I shouted at you earlier.'

'Emma, I didn't mean to be so short with you in the taxi.'

Then a third voice broke into the conversation, breaking the tension.

'Sorry to interrupt.' Mark gave a dry chuckle. 'It seems it's time for apologies all round,' he added, from where he stood beside the table.

Emma glanced at her watch. It was dead on eight o'clock. Mark's timing was spot-on, as always.

'Good evening, Mark.'

She smiled at him, apologetically. Dan got to his feet.

'Evening, Fros—I mean, Mark,' he said, with a concerted effort at civility.

'Evening, er, Daniel,' Mark replied, taking the hand that Dan outstretched towards him, and shaking it briefly. 'What's this? No-one got a drink yet?' Mark asked, sitting down at the table and straightening his cutlery.

'No,' Emma replied, surprised to realise that this was true and she hadn't even noticed. 'Dan and I were too busy talking.'

'Funny, isn't it, Emma, how we never seem to run out of things to say to each other?' Dan said.

Mark glowered. Emma blushed, and cast her eyes down to the wine list. Dan summoned the wine waiter, ordering lagers for him and Mark, a glass of dry white wine for Emma. Another waiter came and took their food orders. Feeling guilty, Emma did not know how to begin to confess things to Mark.

'So, Mark,' she asked politely, instead. 'The receptionist said you were out when Dan and I got back. Did you go anywhere nice?'

Mark wrinkled his nose.

'I'm not sure nice is the word. I visited another zoo, as research for this wretched article I'm supposed to be writing.' His tone darkened. 'Rather than just sit around today and waste my time.'

'Anyway, talking of apologies,' Dan said hastily, as Mark took a sip of his drink, 'I'm well aware that Emma and I owe you one, for leaving you in the lurch today.'

Mark set down his glass. His light blue eyes looked steelier than ever now.

'Ah, yes,' he said calmly. 'I was wondering when you were going to get round to that.'

He looked reproachfully at Emma.

'Don't think I didn't notice you two rushing off first thing this morning. Heavens only knows what the pair of you were up to.'

Emma's eyes filled with sorrow. This was a man she had once had feelings for, but no longer did.

'Sorry, Mark, but we had our reasons. It was imperative that the operation was top secret, that word didn't get out to anyone, even you.'

Mark almost choked on his lager.

'Operation? What operation?'

Emma lowered her voice beneath the din of the dining-room chatter.

'It was to do with the two baby orang-utans I told you about. You know, the ones Dan and I saw that time at the animal market?'

'Yes, I remember,' Mark replied, his whole manner suddenly changing, to that of an eager newshound. 'I want you to tell me everything.'

He reached for something in his jacket pocket, and Emma saw it was his recorder. Mark placed it on the table.

'For goodness' sake, put that thing away!' Dan burst out exasperatedly. Reining in his temper, he sighed. 'I knew it was a mistake for us all to meet up here,' he muttered under his breath. 'I should have put my foot down. We need to talk about this in private, not in the most public place imaginable!'

Emma looked shamefaced.

'Yes, it wasn't one of my better ideas,' she admitted, realising what an error of judgement the rendezvous had been. She turned back to Mark. 'For now, suffice it to say, everything went OK. We were extremely worried about the two animals for a while, but now, fingers crossed, they should pull through.'

'We'll fill you in on all the details,' Dan added, 'in a more appropriate place, at a more appropriate time.' He glanced at Emma. 'First thing tomorrow, maybe.'

With an air of resignation, Mark put his recorder away.

'It's got the makings of a great article,' he admitted grudgingly. 'When you're ready, Fitz—um, Daniel, I'll be happy to write it for you.'

Dan put down his lager glass.

'Thanks, Mark,' he said, sounding genuinely surprised. 'That's very sporting of you.'

There was a pause. Suddenly Dan scraped back his chair, getting to his feet. 'Actually, I've changed my mind about dinner. I think I might eat in my room after all.'

He placed a note on the table.

'That should take care of my share of the bill.'

Emma's eyes widened. 'Dan, why are you leaving?' she asked, shocked.

He glanced from Emma to Mark, and back again.

'I think you two have some talking to do. Three's a crowd, and all that.'

Mark, too, pushed back his chair, getting to his feet.

'No,' he said bluntly. 'If anyone should leave, it's me.' He turned his blue-grey gaze on Emma. 'You're a great girl, and, if the invitation's still open, I'd like, in the future, for us to be friends.'

'Of course, Mark. I'd really like that.'

139

Emma was surprised. Then a warm, grateful smile broke out over her features, like sunshine on a cloudy day. Then Dan spoke.

'I suppose it's too much, uh, Mark,' he began gruffly, facing him across the table, 'to hope that you and I can try to be civil to each other, too.'

'Don't push your luck, Fitzgerald,' Mark said briefly, and with that he was gone, weaving his way amongst the tables and potted palms, before disappearing from view.

Looking a little bemused, Dan sat back down in his chair. For a few moments, Emma just sat, shell-shocked by Mark's sudden exit. Strangely, following his departure, the crackling tension between her and Dan had resumed. There was so much Emma wanted to say to Dan—that he was a kind, brave man, and she loved him—but things were so complicated that she didn't know how to begin.

The waiter brought their starters, glass noodle soup!

'Thank you. This looks delicious.' Dan explained. 'But, unfortunately, one of our party has had to leave early.'

'No problem, sir.'

Bowing politely, the waiter took the third bowl of soup away.

They had only taken a few mouthfuls of their soup when Dan's mobile phone trilled.

Suddenly Emma had lost her appetite and

140

laid down her spoon.

'I hope it's not . . .'

But she couldn't finish her sentence, the words choking her. Her relief had been too hasty, she feared. Rufus had died after all. Dan was reaching for his phone, getting to his feet.

'Excuse me, Emma, I'd better take this call outside in the lobby.'

He rushed off. Emma, impatient for news, thrust down her napkin and rushed after him.

'Dan, wait.'

Panting slightly, she caught up with him in a corner of the lobby.

'Yes,' Dan was saying into the phone. 'Thank you so much for letting me know. That's good news.'

'Well?' Emma demanded as he ended the call.

Dan smiled at her.

'Rufus is off the drip now, and eating a piece of fruit. The vet feels confident he is going to make it.'

Impulsively, Emma flung her arms around him.

'That's fantastic news.'

For a moment they embraced, then pulled back slightly and gazed at each other, as if surprised to be in one another's arms. Then Emma remembered herself and, feeling a little sad and regretful that things were such a mess between her and Dan, pulled away. Still blushing, she cleared her throat.

'So, um, what happens now?'

'Well,' Dan replied, 'I'll keep enquiring as to the orang-utans' progress. Then, when they are fully recovered and quarantined, they will be transferred to a zoo or animal sanctuary.'

'A zoo?' Emma asked, frowning slightly. 'So they won't be released back into the wild?'

Dan shook his head. 'Sadly, animals like those would probably never be able to re-adapt to life in their natural environment.'

'So they end up in a zoo.'

'Yes.' Dan smiled gently, clasping both of Emma's hands. 'And I know of a particularly good one in a little place called Woodhaven, just outside Brighton, in the South of England.'

A wide smile broke out across Emma's mouth.

'So you're going to try and adopt them, are you?' Her heart gave a little leap of excitement. 'Oh, Dan, if you do, please promise me that you'll keep me updated on their progress!'

'That won't be too difficult,' Dan said slowly, looking into her eyes. 'Seeing as I don't intend to let you out of my sight from now on.'

Emma's heart thudded once, twice. Shocked, she allowed herself to be pulled into Dan's arms once again, and kissed with passionate intensity.

When eventually he could speak again, Dan

said huskily, 'I should have believed you that you and Frost were finished, Emma. Now that I realise that there's nothing between the two of you any more, I don't want anything to stand in the way of my feelings for you.'

Startled, Emma somehow managed to form a question.

'Are you sure, Dan?'

Dan looked a little taken aback.

'Of course, Emma. But why do you ask?'

She forced herself to say what she had to say.

'Because, right from the first time when I invited myself along to the animal market with you, I've had the feeling that I'm like an annoying little puppy to you, that keeps following you around, sticking its nose in where it isn't wanted. And that you kept rejecting me, pushing me away.'

Dan laughed softly, his dark eyes shining with emotion.

'I'm sorry if I gave you that impression, Emma, darling Emma, but I can assure you that it couldn't be farther from the truth.'

His kind, gentle eyes crinkled slightly at the corners.

'Maybe I've been such a lone wolf for so long, especially when I'm involved in investigations such as this, that I haven't known how to handle my feelings properly. The truth is, I've fallen in love with you, Emma. And I hope one day to marry you, if you'll have me. What's the matter?' Dan asked suddenly, concerned, gazing down into Emma's face. 'Is it too sudden for you? Trust me to be heavy-handed. I've got no finesse.'

'Oh, Dan,' Emma said quickly, full of joy, voicing those things she hadn't been able to earlier. 'You're a brave, kind man, and I love you. And maybe, one day,' she teased, 'I might even marry you.'

Dan drew her back into his powerful arms and kissed her again, there in the bustling hotel lobby while, back in the restaurant, the waiter stood by an empty table holding two dishes of chicken. A woman's handbag and a man's jacket were still there, and the waiter wondered how two diners could somehow have vanished off the face of the earth!

Chivers Large Print Direct

If you have enjoyed this Large Print book and would like to build up your own collection of Large Print books and have them delivered direct to your door, please contact **Chivers Large Print Direct**.

Chivers Large Print Direct offers you a full service:

✧ **Created to support your local library**

✧ **Delivery direct to your door**

✧ **Easy-to-read type and attractively bound**

✧ **The very best authors**

✧ **Special low prices**

For further details either call Customer Services on 01225 443400 or write to us at

Chivers Large Print Direct
FREEPOST (BA 1686/1)
Bath
BA1 3QZ